down from the Clouds

MARILYN GREY

WINSLET PRESS

WINSLET PRESS

Down from the Clouds
Copyright © 2013 by Marilyn Grey

To learn more about Marilyn Grey, visit her Web site:
www.marilyn-grey.com

Library of Congress Control Number: 2013947493

ISBN-10: 098572353X
ISBN-13: 978-0-9857235-3-8

This novel is a work of fiction. Names, characters, places, and incidents
either are the product of the author's imagination or are used fictitiously.
Any resemblance to actual events, locales, organizations, or persons living
or dead is entirely coincidental and beyond the intent of either the author
or the publisher.

Cover & Interior Design by Tekeme Studios

Printed in the United States of America

First Edition: August 2013
13   12   11   10   9   8   7   6   5   4   3   2   1

To:

*The One I Missed
Across the Sea*

For:

*Showing me that love stories like
this really do exist.*

My Mama always said you've got to put the past behind you before you can move on.
Forrest Gump

"Come, Boy, sit down. Sit down and rest."
And the boy did.
And the tree was happy."
Shel Silverstein, The Giving Tree

To conceal anything from those to whom I am attached, is not in my nature. I can never close my lips where I have opened my heart.
Charles Dickens

Chapter One

She made breakfast for me. Soft, delicate face just as I imagined all those years. Five-feet away from me she twirled on one foot to grab the toffee sauce before spreading it over the steaming chocolate-chip pancakes. Her hair fell in her eyes. She held up her batter-covered hands, laughed at me, and blew the hair away. No special occasion, just us. Like it should've been all my life. She had no idea that within seven hours a ring would be on her finger.

I couldn't stop thinking about it.

And I couldn't stop thinking about all that I gave up for her. Pop was the only man who ever loved me. He told me to leave. To find her. To do whatever it would take.

She set the pancakes down in front of me, next to a single purple rose on my dining room table, then sat down, exhaled, and stared at me. Into me. You'd think we'd known each other for years. Love does that to people.

"I hope it's okay," she said.

I couldn't stop looking at her since the first moment I saw her.

She blushed. "One of these days you'll have to get over the fact that we've found each other."

"Never." I picked up my fork, sliced into the fluffy mountain of yum, and looked at her again. "This will always be a dream to me."

"Well, it's been four months and"—she counted her fingers—"eight days. It's still fresh. You don't think you'll be sick of me one day?"

I laughed. "You trying to ruin our romantic moment with reality?"

"Kind of odd for me now that I think about it."

"I'll never be sick of you. Honestly. I'll never let it happen."

We ate in silence, our eyes speaking to each other across the table as we

Marilyn Grey

shared a plate of food. As we always did. Our friends and family called it puppy love. We called it *us*.

"So," she said. "What's that unopened letter you've been preoccupied with the last few weeks?"

I fidgeted in my seat, made eye contact with the rose. "It's no big deal."

"It's some big deal if you keep staring at it all the time like it's going to bite you."

I didn't want to tell her. Didn't want to tell anyone. Only half of me wanted to open the thing. The other half wanted to throw it out. I didn't want to know what the past had to say to me. Truth is, I left it unopened for months. Flipped it over in my hands, fell asleep with it under my pillow, tossed it out the window only to run after the wind that carried it down the street. Over and over. Like a lunatic.

Matt always said I was mysterious. Everything hidden deep inside like a starving well that hadn't been rained on in years.

Not true.

Rain flooded my well, sometimes overflowing. Only I learned to hide it behind my smile. Who wants to burden others with more issues? Everyone has their own. That's enough. I wanted to bring light and life to people around me. Last thing I wanted was to be a dark and harrowing storm cloud. So I stayed quiet. Hidden. Mysterious, as Matt would say.

And I feared that envelope, sliced open and read, would ruin it for me.

My phone rang. I turned it off without looking. Hard for me to break bad habits. So I try not to start them. Meal times, intimate times, deserved to not be interrupted by screens and beeps.

We finished our breakfast in a comfortable silence.

She stood, cleared the table, and set the dishes in the sink. I followed behind. Wrapped my arms around her, pulled her back into my chest, and ran my fingers to her hands.

"Let me do the dishes," I said. "You can relax in the living room. Matt should be up any minute to serenade us with his piano."

She turned, her cuteness looking up at me. "Ah, the soundtrack of our lives by Matthew Ryan."

"Exactly."

"I heard that," Matt said from his room. His door opened, then shut.

He appeared in the hallway next to the kitchen. "You think Lydia lets me sleep with the wedding being a month away? I get texts and calls even when the crickets are sleeping."

Ella caught me staring at her bare left hand. I smiled. She gave me the eyes. We talked about it so many times before. Since the first week we spent together. We knew we'd spend the rest of our lives together. She didn't understand why I needed to wait to propose. I didn't either. Just knew I wanted it to be special. Right. Not rushed or forced. And of course I had to live up to Matt's proposal. Even he didn't know I was about to propose to Ella. I glanced at the clock. Six hours to go.

ELLA DROVE TO LANCASTER FOR AN AUDITION TO PLAY WITH the Lancaster Symphony Orchestra. I applauded her, encouraged her, then told her I couldn't go. The disappointment in her eyes was enough to break the surprise, but I told myself she would understand when she returned.

I sorted through all of the images I painted, then told Matt he needed to leave.

"Last I checked I still lived here, too," he said.

"Last I checked you were nearly packed up and you spend most of your time in your future wife's apartment."

"True. But what are you planning?"

"Nothing."

"The great and wondrous nothing."

"Of course. Without the great and wondrous nothing I wouldn't be something, now would I?"

"If you say so." He pulled his keys out of his pocket. "I have to go pick out reception decorations with Lydia anyway."

"I thought she didn't want a big wedding?"

"She didn't."

"Women make so much sense."

"That's why we love them. We make sense, they make love."

I laughed. "Nice, but I'm pretty sure they are good for more than that."

"I don't mean sex. I mean love. They teach us how to love and we teach them how to think."

3

"Speak for yourself. I'm thinking Ella will teach me everything. I feel like I have nothing worth giving to this woman. She is seriously the most beautiful person I've ever known."

"I thought that was me?" He hit my back and walked toward the front door. "I'll see ya later. Good luck with your mysterious proposal."

I looked over my shoulder. "I thought I was more clever than that?"

"Apparently not." He smiled and closed the door.

I always wondered if he knew more about me than I thought. Did he know about the letter I refused to read? About the regrets I feared would one day build a wall between Ella and me. My mom's death. My dad's disappearance. Did he know that I blamed myself for all of these things, including the one thing I swore I'd never do? The one thing that kept me from opening that letter and facing what I hated about myself.

I hung the first painting on the apartment door, then stared at it. Bright, summer fun. Blowing bubbles in the backyard by a kiddie pool. I combined our childhood photographs and made it look like we were together as kids. The note on the bottom read: *When most boys dreamed of being a superhero, I dreamed of you.*

I finished placing the rest of the paintings on the floor leading to my room, made chocolate-covered strawberries and brownies, her favorite, and topped it off with a bottle of her favorite wine. Raspberry Eau de Vie. Which quickly became my favorite too. After arranging it all on the living room floor, because, oddly enough, that was her favorite place to have wine and chocolate, I sat on the couch and waited for her call.

The phone rang. I answered, trying not to let my voice shake as much as it wanted to. We talked. About normal things. An entire hour and a half passed until she parked and told me she'd be over in a minute.

I stood, paced the living room, waited. Heart beating right out of my ears, I twirled the ring in my pocket. My mother's ring. The only thing I ever touched that my mother's hand also touched. Ella's exact size. Simple, but elegant. I hoped she'd like it.

Footsteps neared the doorway. Then stopped.

I jogged to my bedroom, cracked the door, and watched her walk in. Smile illuminating her face, she peeked around and saw the next painting on the floor in front of her.

She stopped. Two kids sitting on the swings at school. *When most boys were making fun of girls who hit puberty, I was sitting on the swings wondering if I already knew you and if not, when would I?*

She walked forward. Teenage Ella and Gavin sitting in my old bedroom at Pop's house. *When most guys were counting how many girls they slept with, I was longing for you.*

And the next. Two graduating seniors standing in front of a fork in the road. *When I had to choose between talent and glory or a quiet life with you, I let my dreams of music die and I chose you.*

The next. A boy standing across a coffee shop, hat tilted on top of his messy hair, face dumb and in love with the beautiful girl sitting by the window. The girl. Brown hair pulled into a loose braid over her shoulder, bangs hiding her right eye. She looked at him over her shoulder and smiled. *The day that changed my life.*

And the final painting. Vacant coffee shop. Streetlights glowing on her wet cheeks and lighting her lips. *The night we first kissed and the world around us disappeared. And so ... life begins.*

Hands shaking, I stepped out of my room. Looked at her face and melted. She smiled, tears glossing her eyes. I knelt in front of her, tried to speak, but nothing came out. She took my hand. Kissed it.

"No words, Gavin," she said. "I know."

I looked down. Cleared my throat. "I never had a normal life, Ella. Being found on the side of the road by a stranger isn't the most beautiful beginning." I tried to smile. "So I hid. Most of my life I hid from everyone. And I thought a lot. Sometimes about what I'd be when I grew up, if anything, sometimes about what I'd give to the world, but mostly I thought about you. Maybe I longed for a woman because I never had a mom. Most kids thought I was stupid. Not interested in comic books, I wrote love poems and spent my nights falling asleep to Charles Dickens on tape. I was weird. I don't doubt it at all. These paintings are so real to me because all of this time, all of these years, you were right there with me." I took a breath. "What I'm trying to say is, some people find each other later in life and wonder what it would be like if they could go back and know each other as kids. Grow up together. Fall in love in the sandbox and stay in love through college. But I don't need to do that because all of those times, all of those years, you were right there with me. All because I spent my life dreaming of you. Of this day. Of this second right here."

She shook her head and squeezed my hands.

I squeezed back, took out the ring, and pleaded. "Ella, I want to spend the rest of my life experiencing everything with your hand in mine. I've waited forever for this. Will you marry me?"

She nodded, her eyes hiding under tear-soaked lashes, smile glowing. "Of course, Gavin. Of course."

I stood and slid the ring onto her finger. "I wasn't sure if this would be jinxed or not, having come from my mother's hand before they buried her, but it's the only thing I have of hers and it just seem—"

She pushed her finger over my lips and opened hers. "It's perfect."

"Like you."

"No, like you."

"Like us."

Chapter Two

Friday night, alone in my apartment, Ella and I packed up my past. Matt moved the last of his stuff a few days after I proposed. Weird being without him and being with a woman so much. So fast. Every stroke of the past blended right into the most winsome time of my life. Even the dark blobs of color I didn't want to acknowledge were veiled by soft strands of the present. The soft strands of the beautiful woman staring at the envelope she knew I didn't want to open.

"It's nothing, really," I took it from her hands. Put it in my pocket. "It's just a letter from my grandfather."

"The one who died recently?"

I nodded, slipping the crinkled enveloped further into my pocket. Further from her hands, from my own.

"And why don't you want to read it?" she said.

"It's the last letter he wrote me. I have two others he wrote, but he said to open this one last. The other two were hard enough."

She sat on my bed, perched forward, and tilted her head just so. Almond eyes waiting for me to explain the things I didn't want to share. The things she deserved to know. And would know. Just not yet.

"It's a story for another day," I said.

She bit her lip. "Gavin."

It wasn't a question. I looked down. Away from her eyes. Away from the conflict brewing between us.

"Gavin," she said again.

"Yes?"

She held up her hand. Pointed to the ring I put on it. "I am marrying you. I kinda hoped to marry all of you, not just the pieces you want others to see."

I inhaled and smiled. "Ella, my love."

"Don't say that. Just tell me. Please. I want to know you."

"I want you to know me. Trust me. I'm not hiding."

"Then what are you doing?"

I exhaled so hard I could've blown the little piggies and their brick houses away. "I'm sulking."

She shook her head. "Well, one thing you need to know about me is that I have a hard time letting things go. Especially when people I love are dealing with something inside and don't talk about it. Sarah did this to me all the time. With her it was easy to listen, to be a shoulder, and to have no idea why on earth she was balling her eyes out. With you, I can't pretend I don't want to know. Seeing you hide behind your smile is nice and admirable. I know you don't want to bring others into your problems. But have you ever thought that maybe it would be more admirable to be real in a world that's trained into being fake?"

"I told Matt. He didn't believe me."

"You told Matt what?"

I touched her cheek with the back of my hand. Ran my fingers to her ear. "That you would teach me how to live."

SHE LET THE ENVELOPE GO. FOR NOW. I KNEW SHE'D BRING IT up later, but I needed time.

We pulled up outside of Matt and Lydia's new house. Only Matt lived there so far. Lydia planned to move in after the wedding. Nice little garden, about a half acre of land, solid trees, yellow house with black shutters. It was a nice first house. Small, but nice.

Ella squeezed my hand. I squeezed back, pulled her fingers to my lips, and looked into her eyes. Life never felt so good, so perfect, as it did with her beside me.

"Ready?" She pulled the handle of the car door.

I nodded.

"You okay?"

"I'm fine."

She tried to smile. Not so successful.

I got out of the car and walked over to open her door.

She took my hand. "I want you to know that I desperately want to know what's inside of you. More than I can say. But I'm not going to pry you to open up to me when it's obvious you can't even open up to yourself right now. What am I going to do, though?"

"Yes?"

"I'm going to wait and I'm not going to forget about that envelope."

"I didn't expect you to."

"One day you'll stop hiding. You'll realize how exhausting it is."

We walked toward the soon-to-be Mr. and Mrs. Ryan house. Lydia opened the door.

Matt came up and put his hands on her shoulders. "Look who it is. The newly engaged."

Ella smiled. I kissed the top of her head and pulled her into me.

"Let me see the ring," Lydia said.

"What is it with girls and wanting to show off the ring? Isn't the man even better to show off than a piece of metal and stone?" Matt said, walking into the house. "Gavin, come in and I'll show off my hardwood floors and newel posts."

I laughed and walked past the ladies. "So, Heidi still has no idea she's coming to her baby shower right now?"

"No idea," Matt said from the kitchen.

I followed the trail of his voice. "Hey man, this house is nice. I can't believe how much wood is in this place."

"Yeah, I wasn't kidding when I said hardwood floors. And it's all heart pine. I could rip this stuff up and get rich by selling it."

"If Heidi has no friends here, then who is coming to the shower today?"

"Well, she's met a few of Lydia's friends. When I told Lydia about her she insisted on making her feel welcome and loved. Did you know Heidi is one of the bridesmaids for our wedding?"

"Didn't know. Don't know much about your wedding to be honest. Not even sure I remember the date."

"If I didn't know you better...."

"But you do." I opened the refrigerator and made myself at home by grabbing a beer. "You got the good stuff for me, I see."

"Your favorite. I'd much rather have a root beer any day, but I know how much you like that ale."

I took a sip. "I really do."

Women's voices escalated in the other room. Must've been piling in by the second.

"Are we going to be the only men here?" I said.

"No. Patrick is coming. And Mwenye will be here with Tylissa."

"Wow. This is nice of you guys. I know it's been tough for her. I can't even imagine."

He walked away. I followed him into the living room where a handful of women sat laughing and talking. My Ella knelt on the floor beside the couches. So typical of her. Selfless to the core. She refused to sit until everyone else had a seat and most of the time she ended up standing or sitting on the floor. And I'd follow.

Matt sat next to Lydia on the love-seat. I sat behind Ella and pulled her close. Her hair smelled like a spring morning.

I looked around the room. Didn't recognize anyone yet.

A knock at the door. Ella stood faster than I could've thought to stand. I looked over my shoulder. Tylissa and Mwenye.

I stood. The other women chatted away. So wrapped up in their conversations about shoes and hair that they had no idea the door even opened. Another thing I loved about Ella. Someone's water would be half-filled and she would pour more in before they'd ask. She always thought of others. And the most beautiful thing is I could tell her this a thousand times and she would cock her head at me, roll her eyes, and say, "I didn't do that. Did I?"

She really had no idea. Most of the time, at least. Just in her nature. The way she lived and breathed. So much to admire. Like Jack Nicholson to Helen Hunt. She made me want to be a better man.

I shook hands with Mwenye and gave Tylissa a hug and kiss on the cheek.

"And what's the baby's name again?" I said.

"Asylia," Ella chimed in.

"Swahili, isn't it?" A man's voice said from the doorway.

"Patrick," Ella said, walking to him with her fingers still locked in mine.

"Asylia is beautiful." I followed Ella and nodded for Mwenye's little family to make themselves at home.

I extended my hand to Patrick's, but he pulled me in for a hug. I patted his back and pulled away.

"Congrats on the engagement," he said. "It feels like just yesterday Ella turned me down for some stranger she saw across a coffee shop years before."

I smiled. "Sounds crazy, doesn't it?"

"Crazy in a good way. I told her this would make the news. You guys should write a book or something."

"I'd prefer to live our story instead of writing it," Ella said, eyes on me.

"Come on in," I said. "You've met Heidi before, right? She isn't here yet. It's a surprise. She thinks she's coming for a wedding shower."

"I haven't met her yet," he said. "But having lost a wife to cancer I think I could relate to her a bit."

We walked inside. Everyone stood in mini circles talking with others. Ella hadn't let go of my hand for ten minutes. She led me into the kitchen and smiled, then handed me a pitcher of water and a plastic cup. I looked at her. She motioned toward Tylissa. Ah, nursing mother needed a drink. Leave it to Ella.

I poured a cup of water, spritzed a lemon in, positioned it on top of the cup, and walked toward Tylissa. Ella crossed her arms in the kitchen and smiled. I loved that we could have conversations without opening our mouths. Sometimes we'd sit in front of each other with blindfolds and talk to each other with our hands. Dangerously sensual. I only recommend it if you're truly in love, something so amazing shouldn't be wasted on just anyone.

Tylissa thanked me for the drink, downed it in thirty seconds flat, and handed it back. I laughed and turned to Ella.

"She's here," someone said.

We huddled together and waited for her to knock on the door. Matt answered and ushered her in.

"Surprise!"

Heidi covered her mouth with her hands, looked around the room, and caught the pink and white streamers and those little decorative cakes the girls made with a set of diapers. Her hand fell beside her.

"I can't believe this," she said, then walked to each person in the room to thank them with a hug.

Ella gave her a warm hug and made her way to the kitchen. I stood beside Matt and watched Ella out of the corner of my eye. I couldn't get enough of her. Wanted to stand beside her every second I could.

I refrained. Stayed near Matt and listened to Heidi talk about the crazy requests of her in-laws.

"I'm not trying to be difficult," she said. "I really want to have a relationship with them, especially since I don't with my own parents. But it just seems like they don't want me around. If I weren't pregnant I have no doubt they would never speak to me again."

"I can relate to that," Patrick said from behind her.

She turned.

"Oh, sorry." He looked down. "I didn't mean to listen to your conversation. You guys just happened to be right behind me."

"Oh, are you Jenna's husband?" Heidi said.

"No, my wife died not too long ago from cancer. And the reason I can relate to you is because the cancer went to her brain, affected her mental health to the point that she ended up like a vegetable." He exhaled, took a breath, and steadied himself on the wall beside him. "It was me who decided to cut off life support. Her parents say I'm a murderer."

Heidi's smiled disappeared like the sun hidden by a marshmallowy sky, then it appeared again. "They can say what they want, but I can tell you loved her and you only wanted the best for her." She touched his shoulder. "I would've done the same."

Matt and I looked at each other. Lydia walked over to help Ella in the kitchen. Matt followed her. I stood there for a second, watching Patrick and Heidi's conversation find its way to the couch, then made my way back to my soon-to-be wife.

She smiled when I came in the room. I leaned into the refrigerator and shrugged toward the living room. "Looks like Heidi and Patrick are pretty deep in conversation."

Matt laughed. "Yeah, I'll say."

Lydia handed Matt a tray of snacks to take to the dining room table. Ella took a water to Heidi, sat beside her and Patrick, looking like a ballerina in a monster truck show. Completely out of place.

She came back to me, pulled me aside, and whispered in my ear, "We have to stop them."

I leaned in. "Stop who?"

"Patrick and Heidi." Her green eyes darkened. "They can't be interested in each other. She still has her ring on. They're still married in spirit."

I smiled. "Ella, have you ever though that maybe it could be just as romantic to fall in love again after something so tragic?"

"Well, Jack died and Rose moved on after the Titanic, but that's not my idea of happily ever after."

"Maybe it's theirs."

She crossed her arms. "It can't be."

"Don't be so childish," I said, joking.

She walked away. Our sweet love story gone south too soon. I followed after her.

Matt grabbed my arm. "Seriously, man? Practice your sarcasm on me. Not her. Now you're in for it."

I pinched the bridge of my nose to prevent the impending headache. "I'm stupid, what can I say?"

ELLA TRIED HER BEST TO AVOID ME THROUGHOUT THE REST of Heidi's shower. I couldn't tell if she was more interested in breaking Heidi and Patrick up or making me feel sorry for myself. Whatever it was, she only succeeded in one. Heidi and Patrick were inseparable the entire night and exchanged phone numbers at the end.

Maybe what I said sounded mean and sarcastic, and I was joking, but seriously? I happened to desire Ella and Ella only. If she died I'd bury my heart with her and never dig it up for someone else. But I don't and never will place those expectations on another person.

She sat in the car. I closed her door and walked to mine. Cool breeze followed me, rustling trash in the gutter and scaring off a wild rabbit. Stars were bright. Sky opened up like a planetarium. I sat down and looked at my bright star turned black cloud. She stared out the window as I started the car and accelerated.

"I'm sorry," I said.

She didn't budge.

"Ella, forgive me. I'm stupid. I really am. I hope I didn't hurt you. I was joking, but at the same time I do believe that you need to let them live their lives and accept whatever happens. You can't control people around you."

"Easy for you to say," she said, still looking out the window. "This coming from the man who tucks everything so far inside and won't open up to his fiancé."

"That's me. I don't want pity from people, but if someone around me wants to stand on a soap box and get a pity party together to try and wrangle in some trivial flattery, I'm not going to stop them. Whether I think it's ridiculous or not, it doesn't matter. It's not my life."

She finally turned to me. "Would you remarry someone if I died?"

"No."

"Then why do you think it's so romantic to fall in love after the love of your life is buried?"

I reached for her hand. She took it. I exhaled. Relieved.

"I don't think that. Ella. Not in the slightest. I don't know what their life will entail and I don't know either of them well enough to know what's best for them. What I do know is that Heidi almost had an abortion because her baby has some kind of condition or deformity of the leg and absolutely no one in her life to help take care of this child. I won't blame her for falling in love with another man. And I won't blame him either."

"But it was so romantic of her to keep her ring on for him. I can't imagine her taking it off."

I smiled. "Sweetheart, don't think so much." I pointed to her chest. "Worry about what's in here." And pointed to mine. "And in here. That's all that matters. We're all that matters to us. The rest of the world can write their love stories as they see fit. Let's just worry about writing our own."

She smiled. Ah, success. I said the right thing. Nothing short of a miracle.

Her eyes widened as she reached for the dashboard. I looked ahead.

Something crashed into my windshield and rolled off the hood. I swerved, lost control of the car, and ended up on the other side of the road facing the wrong direction. Shaking, I gathered my thoughts and looked at Ella. Lost in panic, she hit my leg.

"Get back on the right side of the road," she said, looking out the window for whatever it was that hit my car.

Please don't let it be a person, I thought. Then moved the car and parked on the other side of the road. Ella jumped out of the car and paced along the white line. I couldn't move. Looked in my rear view. She shook her head and held back tears. I sunk into my seat and imagined the worst.

Tears in her eyes, she appeared beside me. I got out and looked behind the car.

"It's a baby," she said.

I looked around and spotted the mother behind a tree, eyeing the mangled baby deer as he twitched to his death. I thought of my own mother. The fear she must have experienced. The pain. The torture of handing me over as she lay dying on a sterile hospital bed.

"Is there anything we can do?" Ella said.

"I don't think so."

She knelt beside the little deer. "Poor thing."

I looked at the mom. "Um, love. You may not want to get too close. In fact, maybe we should go so his mom can come closer. She won't come near him with us standing here."

Ella nodded. We got back in the car. I called the cops and my insurance company while she perched herself backwards on her seat and watched the deer as we drove off.

"Hey," I said. "I want to tell you a little about my past."

She pulled my hand to her lap.

"Just so you know, I've never told anyone this. Not even Matt."

She nodded. Smiling with her eyes. Telling me in her silent gaze that I was safe with her. I could pour my heart out and she would drink what so many others would spit back out and lather with their pity.

Pity I didn't want.

"My mom was given a choice when she was pregnant. They told her most likely I would die and she would die if she tried to deliver me. She

21

refused the abortion. My dad begged her to abort me. So, when I was born it turned out that I didn't have any complications, but Mom did. She died and my dad took me from the hospital. Everyone said he handled it so well. But someone found me on the side of the road with the hospital birth card and footprint papers tucked in the car seat. My pop eventually got custody of me and my dad has been missing since. Harold Kessler. Missing person for over two decades. His body has never been found. No death records. He's just gone."

She kissed my hand and held it against her lips.

"My pop is my dad's father. So I learned a lot about my dad through him, but not my mom. Her parents died when I was five and seven. Never knew them well since they lived in Texas. Pop was all I had." I parked the car in the parking garage and leaned back. "Until you."

"You've had Matt. He's your best friend. That's gotta count for something."

"It does. And while I know him and I are close, I doubt he loves me unconditionally. If I ruined his life he would leave, too. Just in our current culture's nature to run from pain and problems. There are few people who will love you no matter what. Pop was that for me. And now you."

"Well, in that case I've never had anyone love me like that until you. I hope I can be that for you, Gavin. I fear myself. I fear my inability to love you more than I love my own self. My reaction to Heidi and Patrick showed me that. It showed me that I love my own ideals more than I love people."

"And you fear that when you come down from the clouds and life doesn't look so bright anymore that you will run off looking for another plane to send you soaring above."

"Exactly."

"But every plane lands."

"Yes." She turned her gaze away from me. "Yes, they do."

"So let's pinky swear."

She laughed. "I haven't done that since elementary school."

I linked my pinky finger with hers. "I swear to land my plane on your heart and learn to live there. For better or worse and way past when death parts us. I will never look for another plane to fly."

Her smile brightened the dimmed car. "And I swear to let to go of my ideals and learn to make reality even more beautiful than the fantasies Disney has given me."

I laughed and pulled her into me. There, in the orange glow of parking garage lights, we kissed and held each other until the windows fogged. I took her hand and wrote the date on the window, enclosed by a heart, and imprinted both of our pinkies inside.

I had never loved anything as much as the girl in my arms. And it felt good, so good, to know that she felt the same.

Chapter Three

The next few weeks flew by. Ella and I settled on a house in the city. Opposite of Matt and Lydia who fled the busy town for suburbia. After tons of discussion, Ella and I decided to do the same, but we fell in love with a four-bedroom city house built in 1890. Still loads of original features. Amazing detail in the wood. Three fireplaces that actually worked. A huge kitchen Ella could dance in as she served waffles and yogurt. Our favorite breakfast. Since the first moment we stepped inside the house we knew we wanted it. And a few weeks later we stood outside holding the key.

"I can't believe life is changing so much so fast." She stood by the door, waiting for me to open it.

I turned the key and pushed the door open. "Home."

She walked inside with a smile painted to her ears. "If I were the squealing type I'd definitely be squealing right now."

"Please don't."

We laughed. Bare walls and floors. Eager to hold life again. I always wondered how interesting it would be to see life from the perspective of an old house. To see the tears and smiles and hard work that lives and breaths inside the walls for decades. To watch from a distance as life goes on and people move out, only to slap on a fresh coat of paint for the next family to cover with their memories.

I couldn't wait to share a home with my Ella. We thought we'd wait to have kids until we moved out of the city, but since she refused to use birth control pills after Sarah's cancer scare there wouldn't be any way to stop the kiddos from coming. I didn't mind though.

Ella sat indian-style on the hardwood living room floor. "It seems like just yesterday I was in Tylissa's house admiring her family pictures. Her growing belly. All that she had. And thinking I'd never have it for myself."

"And here we are." I sat down beside her.

"Funny thing. She asked me to write a list of everything I wanted in a future husband. When I gave it to her she ripped it up and told me no one can live up to lists like that. To let go of my expectations and see what happens."

"I'd love to see that list."

"Wouldn't be hard."

"I thought she ripped it up?"

"She did. But it's still in my head." She tapped my temple. "And it's you. Everything in the list is you."

"Are you serious? Like what?"

"I really am serious. I said I wanted someone with dark hair. Tall, but not too tall. Someone who plays an instrument, sings in the shower, and can be quiet for hours without a single need to speak. Someone with artistic talent of some kind, or at least an appreciation of the arts. Funny. Not into sports. Not a big alcohol guru. I can't remember everything. It was a long list. But trust me, she thought I'd never find someone to meet my expectations, and honestly Gavin, you're so much more than I imagined."

I traced her jaw with my fingertips, stopped on her chin, just below her shiny lips. Woman. There's nothing like a woman. Stripped down from the world's air-brushed, make-upped, faked-up ideals, woman, to me, meant comfort. She defined love, solace, dreams, and beauty all wrapped up in one package. There were times I wondered if I'd ever have a woman to call my own. Searching for Ella seemed like an impossible task. Girl walks into a coffee shop and spots me across the way. I get caught up in customers and orders and an extremely urgent need to run to the bathroom before I embarrass myself, only to come back and see an empty chair.

I told myself I'd find her. Ran out the door that night. Up and down the street. Nowhere. Pop told me to keep trying. To never give up. He said, "When you know you know, and when I met your grandmother the world stopped. That's how you know it's the lady you want to spend the rest of your life with. When the world stops and all you see is her."

Ella's voice carried my thoughts away.

"What'd you say?" I said, taking her hand in mine.

"What are you thinking?"

"Just about you. That night I first saw you and thought I'd never see you again. My pop telling me to never give up. To fight until I bled to find you. And then searching for years to no avail, wondering if I was ridiculous. Watching Braveheart one too many times with Matt. Feeling this ache because while all of those William Wallace speeches were amazing, the thing I could never get out of my head was that all of those things he did, it was all for her. The one he loved. The one they took from him. He fought so hard for her. I wanted someone to fight for too. But you were beginning to feel like a fantasy, not real life." She reclined in my lap and looked up at me. I ran my fingers through her hair, down her neck. "I was so close to giving up."

"Good thing I let that news lady interview me that night."

"I came home that night from a long day of feeling like a nobody. Matt and Lydia were all curled up on the couch. I was happy for them, but man did I wish they were on her couch instead. Then I saw your face. I knew right away. When I ran out the door I felt like a roller-coaster just about to tip over the biggest hill."

She sat up and faced me. Inches from my face. The love of my life. I waited for her to lean in. To let me love her. But she stayed there, her sweet minty breath on my lips, looking into my eyes, to a place no one had ever seen before.

She saw through my mask. No one except ole Pop could do that. And even he couldn't give me chills like Ella could. One glance of her eyes is all it took. And this was far more than a glance.

I broke eye contact. Looked down at her chest, rising and falling so close to mine.

"What's in the envelope?" she said, eyes still on me.

"The envelope? Can't we have a romantic moment where we talk about our storybook beginning and how we want to have two boys and two girls and keep the story going?"

"This is romantic to me. Getting to know you. Seeing you dig up things you've kept inside because no one climbed deep enough to pry it out of you. I'm climbing. And I'll keep climbing until I free whatever part of you that you've hidden from the rest of us."

"You are a determined one, aren't you?"

"I am known for that."

We smiled.

"I'm really not hiding anything. I told you about my mom and dad. That's pretty much everything."

"Except that envelope."

"Well, even I don't know what's in that."

"Don't you think it's time you did?"

"No."

She laughed. "Can I read the first two he wrote you?"

"If you want."

"I do."

"Okay."

THINGS GOT CRAZY WITH MATT AND LYDIA'S WEDDING. ELLA was a bridesmaid and the cake maker. I was the best man and cake maker's taste tester. Before we had much time to blink the wedding snuck up on us, giving Ella enough distractions to forget about the envelopes from Pop. I knew the time would come eventually, but I really didn't want to explain why one of my biggest regrets in life involved her.

Ella and I parted ways to get ready for the wedding. Her best friend Sarah picked her up since she was asked to be the photographer. And she's a great photographer. We met in art school and became good friends. I still can't believe Ella was right there all along. I'm not one for believing in God, but the way life was orchestrated sometimes, well, it really made me wonder.

I arrived at Matt's house before anyone else. Like a good best man should. He opened the door happier than a kid on his birthday.

"It's about time you and Lydia tie the knot." I walked inside and shut the door.

"I wrote a song for her. I'm going to play it as she walks down the aisle. She has no idea."

"She'll love it. She's been wanting you to write a song for her since the day she first saw you play."

"I know. I just had too many issues."

"Yes. And now that this is all in the past, can you look back and figure out why on earth you had issues marrying a beautiful woman who loves you more than anyone else ever has?"

We sat on the couches across from each other. He spread his legs and tapped his knee.

"Well," he said. "Probably my lack of commitment and decision skills, mixed with a little bit of fear."

"Fear of what?"

"The unknown and the too familiar."

"And that means?"

"The unknown would be having kids, paying bills, being stuck with other people to care for and a self-employed business that has its bad months."

"And the too familiar?"

"Growing so used to someone and fearing I might wake up one day and realize I'm bored and want a change."

I nodded. "Interesting."

Someone knocked on the door. Matt stood. "Hey, I'm honest."

"That's true."

"You mean you never think that?"

"Not in the slightest."

"Man, and I thought I had ideals."

He opened the door. His family came in and hugged him. I waited, then stood to greet them. His mom hugged me and whispered, "I'm so happy for you too." His dad shook my hand without much emotion and walked into the dining room, out of sight. Most awkward person I've ever met. You wonder how the man had children when he can't seem to shake a person's hand without beelining for the soap.

Matt's older brother, Michael, shook my hand. "Nice seeing you again. Been a while."

"Yeah," I said. "How's everything going?"

"It's going."

His younger sister, Miranda, patted my back and gave me a hug. "Gavin, I can't believe it's been so long."

"Hey, Miranda. I know. I've been so busy. It's really no excuse."

"Oh, I go by Randy now."

"Is that to match your new orange hair?"

"My hair changes almost weekly. I have to keep it exciting."

"I can see that. Must take after Matt, huh?"

"Why do you say that? Matt's about as boring as it gets."

I laughed.

"This is my boyfriend." She pointed to the guy beside her, complete with high-water skin tight jeans and, why yes, it appeared to be makeup on his face.

I extended my hand. "Gavin."

"I'm Kennedy." He shook my hand and practically cut off my blood flow.

"So, Mira—I mean, Randy. What's with the new name? Trying to escape from the ties of Miranda and turn into a super hero?"

"Eh." She laughed. "I like to think of it as growing. An adult has strong, huge bones compared to a baby. While they may be the same bones you had since birth, they sure do look different."

"Interesting. I guess I see the point."

"Don't strain too hard," she said. "Might hurt yourself."

Matt walked over with his youngest brother, Max, who stared off behind me as he twiddled his thumbs.

"Max, buddy. How's it been?"

He tried to smile. Made a sound, then jumped up and down.

"How old are you going to be next week?" I said, noticing the Lion King book in his hands.

"Tell Gavin how excited you are for your sixteenth birthday," Matt said, knowing as well as I did that Max stopped talking when he turned three and hadn't made a peep since.

Smiling and putting Simba as close to his eyes as possible, he jumped in place again. I gave him a hug. He accepted, but didn't hug back. The only way Max expressed love was in his smile and the way he jumped up and down or banged hangers together. That meant happiness. Sadness or frustration generally involved banging his head on the nearest hard surface or ripping something into a thousand pieces at a frantic pace. I only saw that happen twice and I felt hopeless. Can't imagine how Mrs. Ryan must have felt.

She walked back over. "Well, boys. Ready for the big day?"

Matt smiled. "As long as Gavin doesn't lose the ring, we're good."

"And that is likely." I checked my pocket to make sure. "You know me well."

I STOOD FACING ROWS OF EAGER FACES. THEY CHOSE A beautiful place to get married. It used to be an old mansion, but someone bought it and turned into an overly romantic wedding ceremony and reception place. The entire ceiling on the top floor was removed and replaced with a glass ceiling, along with glass walls. The star-filled December sky and the Philadelphia skyline was all you could see. I looked around the room, lit only be the soft glow of candles. Amazing how candlelight could warm even the hardest faces.

Matt's foot shook under his piano bench as the flower girls walked to the sound of my gorgeous Ella playing the violin. She wore deep red down to her ankles like the bridesmaids who came in after the girls. Hair down, curled, and pearl earrings dangling from her left ear. She alway had her hair behind her left ear, never the right. The bridesmaids positioned themselves across from us and Lydia stood at the white and red rose-laden opening meant to be the door.

She looked like Arwen in *Lord of the Rings*. Poet sleeves hung to the floor. Long crinkled dress flowed far behind her and followed her as she moved. Wavy hair to her elbows. Smile catching the tears dripping from her eyelashes. I never understood why women spent so much money and time on their makeup for their wedding when they ended up washing it off before they even got to the groom.

Matt smiled as his fingers graced the keys and his voice echoed through the room.

I found myself surrounded by darkness,
and the future looked so grim.
It was as if someone turned the light off

and I didn't know where to begin.
I was falling at every turn,
looking for your smile,
but I hadn't seen the truth and light
till I looked back in your eyes.

Can you take the hand of this blind man?
With you I can finally see.
With our hands held together,
we will walk in harmony.
And if I ever loose my way again
I'll know just where to turn.
Back to you my guiding light
for you, my sweet one, this heart of mine does yearn.

And now that we are standing together
with our life about to begin,
I can feel the warmth of the sun shine on
with open hearts the love floods in.
As I stand with you face-to-face,
looking at your smile,
I know nothing else could be this right.
Our future starts tonight.

Can you take the hand of this blind man?
With you I can finally see.
With our hands held together
we will walk in harmony.
And if I ever loose my way again
I'll know just where to turn.
Back to you my guiding light
for you, my sweet one, this heart of mine does yearn.

Let's away my love,
Let the world fade fast.

Down from the Clouds

I'll swear by heaven above,
this love of ours will last.

Now … take the hands of this blind man,
to you I pledge my life,
to love you faithfully,
I'm counting myself as blessed to call you my wife.

Lydia stopped three feet away from me, kissed her dad on the cheek, and left his arm to join Matt's. He stood from the piano and took her hands. His smile could've broken his jaw if it were any wider. Lydia couldn't stop crying, but I can't tell you much after that because my eyes never left the picture of Ella standing across from me, staring right back.

She stood beside the bridesmaids, hands clasped in front of her, green eyes shining in the candlelight. I smiled at her and mouthed, "I love you." She held up her pinky and mouthed, "I love you more."

During the rest of the ceremony the world disappeared as I stared at the most beautiful thing to walk into my life. I couldn't wait to marry her.

To call her my own.

Chapter Four

While Matt and Lydia spent their honeymoon on the hills of New Zealand—yes, a tribute to *Lord of the Rings*—Ella and I bought new furniture for our house and picked paint colors for every room.

I have to say—and I'm not bragging here (well, maybe a little)—it amazed me how we agreed on so many things. I always imagined arguments or disagreements when it came time to decorate a house with my new wife, but not with Ella. Honestly, it was probably because she didn't care about that kind of thing. The complete opposite of Lydia in every way, but now that I thought of it, she reminded me a lot of Matt.

Interesting.

I shook the thought and turned to Ella. "I can't believe you don't have more of an opinion about the house considering your skills with Chances."

She shrugged. "It's kind of like my face. I can make it look better if I want to, but there's rarely a moment that I want to."

I laughed. "Unique way of life there. Not sure many women could relate."

"Well, as long as you don't care, I definitely don't."

"I like your natural beauty. I'd take real over accentuated beauty any day."

"Not sure many men could relate to you either, then. You'd never miss the fact that your guy friends would never consider your wife sexy?"

"Pssh . . . are you kidding me? You've always said I'm the only man that should see that side of you, and I can't help but love that idea."

She kissed my cheek. "You're a sweet one. If I didn't know better I'd say you were a good liar."

"There's not much I'm good at, to be honest."

"Oh, right. You can't fake humility with me. You're paintings are better than Monet, your music writing skills are way better than anything on the radio"—she twirled around the room—"your house decorating abilities. There's so much. Not to mention you are quite handsome."

I took her hand. "Dance with me."

My phone beeped. She looked up at me as we slow danced under the chandelier in the empty dining room. My phone beeped again.

"You can get it," she said.

"You know how I feel about letting technology interfere with life."

It beeped again.

"Might be important."

"Nothing is important enough."

I took it out to silence it and saw a bazillion missed calls from Matt. Not like him to call so much. They must've been back already.

"It's Matt," I said. "Maybe I will call him back. Is that okay?"

"More than okay."

She unpacked a box as I dialed.

"Gavin," he said. "Did you see the news?"

"What news? Are you back already?"

"We're on the way home from the airport. When we were there I saw something on the news. You never told me your dad went missing."

"You never asked."

"Well, he's not missing anymore."

My stomach rose to my mouth. I waited to hear those words since I was five. Other dads dropped their kids off at school, taught them to ride a bike, tie their shoes, and fly kites. Not mine. He disappeared and chose to desert me. I told myself I'd never let him back in. I wished he were dead. I didn't want him to show up again. I didn't want to face what he did to me. I didn't want a dad.

"Are you sure it's him?"

Ella stopped and looked up at me.

"Has to be. He said he came back because of his dad's health and he wanted to meet his son, who happens to be named Gavin Kessler."

"Okay."

"We'll talk later. Check the news."

"I'd rather not."

"How do you feel about it?"

"I don't."

"Right. The ever mysterious wonder."

We hung up and Ella inched toward me. "Your dad is back?"

"Apparently."

"And you don't want to meet him?"

"No."

She sensed my defensiveness. I didn't want to take it out on her. Didn't want her to see the anger and bitterness I held inside because of that man, that man who decided after three decades of lost memories he was going to show up and apologize and have a son again? No way in hell.

Ella touched my arm, kissed my neck, and whispered in my ear. "I'm here if you want to talk."

I didn't. "I'm sorry. I just don't think I want to give him the honor of being talked about."

She pressed her cheek against mine and wrapped her arms around my neck. "I love you."

"I love you, too."

THERE ARE MANY SIDES TO ALL OF US. THERE'S THE SIDE WE show the world. The one that cleans up a messy house before guests arrive, but not for our own spouse. The one that holds a phone in front of our faces for hours, snapping a thousand pictures until we find one good enough for Facebook. This is the side we want others to see. Then there's the real side of us. The side of us buried inside that few people find. Some of us pretend to reveal our true colors. We pride ourselves in being "authentic" and "transparent," touting our flaws like there's no tomorrow, except we choose the flaws we want to show the world in our "transparency." What a joke, really.

Then there's the side no one knows, not even ourselves. The side we suppress and shove so deep inside that we forget about it. Meeting this side of myself didn't appeal to me. Scared the life out of me. I didn't want to find flaws I didn't know existed. Real flaws that I didn't want to parade around. These are the things that make us who we are, the very things we want to hide from everyone around us as we pretend to be someone else. Someone we wish we could be, and all the while miss out on living our own life, real life.

I don't know about you, or anyone else for that matter, but for me it felt safe to hide behind the person I wished I could be. It was easier. Joy could be turned on like a light switch. I liked life this way. The idea of my boat being shaken by a storm at sea didn't appeal to me. Ye of little faith.

That's me.

I didn't want to change, but when a quick-talking detective called to ask if I'd like to set up a day to reunite with Harold Kessler I knew there would come a time when choice no longer existed. Change was about to grip me by the neck and shake me until I consented.

I said, "No, thank you," and hung up the phone. How can you reunite with someone you were never united to in the first place?

Ella walked in the door a few minutes after I hung up the phone.

"What happened?" she said, closing the door.

"Detective called."

"A detective? For what?"

"To reunite me with my long lost father. What do they think this is? Some kind of Hallmark special?"

She reached for my hand. "Calm down. I've never seen you act like this."

There. It happened. The flaws underneath bubbled at the surface, desperate to erupt. I shoved them back inside. Smiled. Pulled her into my body and hid my face in her hair.

"Let's get married now."

"I want to do things properly, Gavin. You know that. I want the first time we sleep in this house together to be when we come back from our honeymoon. And I want our wedding to be something we remember with fondness, not something rushed because we want to turn the page."

"You are a modern Jane Austen, huh?"

"Trying to be."

"Most people are living together without getting married nowadays."

"Not interested." She pulled away from my arms and forced me to look into her eyes. Her finger pressed into my lips. "I know when these things produce real smiles. And I know when they're fake."

I sat on our new white couch. "Come here."

She sat on the opposite side of the couch and draped her feet over my legs. I rubbed her ankles and battled whether to give her the letter in my pocket. I carried all three letters with me every day. Only took them out of my pocket to wash my pants.

"Let me read the first one." I'm not sure whether I loved or hated that she read my mind. Maybe both, depending on the circumstance.

I pulled the first two letters from my pocket. Those stayed in my back left pocket, while the unopened one lived in my right pocket. Alone. Not a single tear in the seal.

"Count to three, take a deep breath, and hand it to me."

"There's something I need to tell you first."

Chapter Five

After a long and exaggerated breath, I looked at her and searched for the words to say what I felt. That didn't always come easy to me. A lover of words and books, sometimes too many letters clamored my brain. I couldn't piece them together into something nice. I needed to try though. For her sake. So, I opened my mouth to tell her what only half of me wanted to say.

"Ella," I said, hands sweating. "When I saw you in that coffee shop my life changed. In middle school and my first year of high school people thought I was the biggest geek ever. Around my junior year I stopped hiding behind books and paint brushes and pretended to be fun and outgoing. I didn't actually have fun and I was still shy inside. All the girls thought I was some kind of god, and occasionally I'd use them to satisfy some bruised part of my ego, but it all got old. I hated that life.

"Then I saw you. That moment changed my life. I realized that I didn't want to party and drink beer while standing on my head. I didn't want to use girls who were just as broken as I was. I wanted life.

"When you smiled at me from the table by that window, you showed me . . . I can't even find the words. All I know is I wanted to be a better man than I was. I wanted to be me. Myself. The part of me hidden inside that no one saw. And I wanted someone to love me for that person, not the person I pretended to be."

"You know," she said. "I feel the same. Except when I saw you I went a little crazy. Because of the car accident and my lack of organization, I lost so much. So I set out to become as organized and detailed as possible. I thought it would help me find you. If I made every choice with precision everything would be perfect. I'd find you. And it would all be wonderful.

Marilyn Grey

Only it didn't work. You found me because everything around me fell apart. I actually had to lose the Ella I had been and resurrect the Ella that died in order for love to find me. It's almost as though I wasn't ready. When I finally let go of my obsession with finding you, you came to me."

"Well. I tend to hide a lot. Have since I was a kid. Honestly, Ella, I'm scared to death at the things buried inside of me. I know it will be liberating to get these things out, but I don't know where to start."

"Start with the letters in your hand."

"Yes. Back to that. So, I wanted to find you. I had to find you. Pop told me to do whatever it took, but I thought it was crazy and useless. So I went off to college and Matt broke up with his girlfriend at the time. For some reason, that made me think of you and how I wanted to find you. Pop's health took a turn for the worse so I went back to Lancaster to live with him. I'd visit Philly every weekend to look for you. Told everyone but Pop that I had art shows.

"Eventually he told me to move back to Philly. Matt needed a room-mate and Pop knew how much I wanted to be there. I believed I'd never find you. I thought I'd end up single until I was forty or settling for less than the dream of you. Pop never thought that."

"He sounds like a modern day Jane Austen, too."

I tried to smile. "He was a lot like you."

"So, he made you come to Philly to find me and how does that lead to these letters?"

"His health got worse. I got really depressed. Didn't tell Matt. Didn't tell anyone. My grandfather was all I had. The thought of him dying scared me. I didn't know love outside of him and thought I never would. So I ignored him."

"You stopped talking to him when you found out he was dying?"

"He sent me a letter. It's the first one here." I placed it in her lap and hung my head on the back of the couch.

She opened it. Paper crinkled as I watched the chandelier cast shadows and bursts of light on the walls around us.

I read every word in my mind as I imagined her eyes scanning them.

42

Down from the Clouds

Dearest Gavin,

You know I consider you my son. I want you to know that I made a lot of mistakes in my life. I wasn't a good dad and your father's issues are because of me. It's the one regret I have in my life. Not raising him better. Not being the father I should have been. I couldn't fix your grandmother when she went to the psych ward, and I certainly couldn't fix myself either. I was a mess, my boy. And messes create more messes until someone starts cleaning. Unfortunately I didn't start cleaning until your dad left and you landed in my arms. But it was too late. He was gone.

I've tried my best, Gavin. Please know it. I've tried my best to raise you, but I've always felt like I wasn't enough. I couldn't be your father no matter how much I taught you to play hopscotch or trace constellations in the sky. I couldn't fill the void you had.

I know you try so desperately to hide the tiniest amount of pain and because of that you hide your emotions too. You're afraid to love because you think love will bring loss and you can't bear it. It's the reason you want to find this girl and never marry someone else if something happened to her. You fear losing things.

I'm dying, Gavin. They say I have a month to live, or less. **Do not live your life based off of fear.** *If you marry this girl and stay faithful to her for life, do it out of love. Not fear. If you do it out of fear, you're a selfish coward. If you do it out of love, you're a noble hero.*

I know you fear my death, but please come and see me before I die. You'll regret it if you don't.

I love you,
Your Ole Pop

Marilyn Grey

I WISH I COULD READ PEOPLE LIKE ELLA. I WANTED TO KNOW what she was thinking, but she didn't tell me. She read the letter, put it back in the envelope, and curled up on my chest until 1:23am. I know because I didn't sleep. I stared at her and the clock, wondering what she thought of me. I knew she loved me, but she signed up for romance, not a mess.

She left that night without saying much. I figured she expected I'd talk when I wanted to. Or maybe she didn't know what to say.

Days later we went shopping for a wedding dress. She wanted something simple. Something resembling the 1920's. Something that would cost us no more than a hundred beans.

I loved that about her.

Not the money thing. The simplicity. The fact that she could take something old and make it beautiful. Maybe she'd do that with me.

"They say it's bad luck for the groom to see the bride's dress before they marry." She peeked through the dressing room in the back of a dingy vintage shop.

"That must mean you like it."

She stepped out. Her cheeks flushed with pink as she stood on her tippy toes and looked down. Soft, white dress from days gone by draped to her knees, hitting her curves in all the right places. "You like?"

Words, tangled up in knots, stayed in my heart and never made it to my mouth. Not like it mattered. Ella and I spoke best when we didn't use words. Our eyes could say so much more. So I used my eyes to show her how I felt. She blushed even more, then slid behind the door and laughed.

I bought the dress for her and we stepped outside. Cold city air stung our noses. I inhaled. Fumes from cars mixed with the fresh scent of snow. The grey evening welcomed us. Delicate snow flakes dusted the high buildings and slushy streets, turning every color into a world of white. I buried my nose in my scarf and pulled Ella into me. She wrapped her scarf around her head and nuzzled against my shoulder.

"Where'd we park?" I said through layers of warm fabric.

She looked up and shrugged.

I smiled. "Great."

A rush of wind blew a newspaper quite a few blocks away. As it flipped and flopped into the frosty air, I kissed my love. Mid-kiss the nice snow flakes turned into freezing rain. She laughed. I probably looked like a frantic homeless man as I wrapped my scarf around my face, looked back and forth, and bolted toward wherever I thought I had parked.

Ella's hand in mine, we ran through the city looking for my car. I saw it a few blocks over and across the street. She could barely keep up because of her laughter, so I picked her up and carried her in my arms as I ran full-speed across the street and, why yes, like any prince charming would, I slipped on the curb. We fell in a puddle of mud, sleet, and snow. Ella's dress flew out of the bag and into the middle of the street. A cab swished by, splashing the dress with specks of brown and grey.

I ran and picked it up, then jogged back to Ella and slipped again, this time landing on my back because I didn't want to ruin the dress even more.

"Stop laughing," I said, trying not to laugh myself. "I hate the cold. I'd rather sit in a stove and burn to death than be outside in this."

Bent over in tears and laughter, she grabbed my scarf and pulled me to her. "Kiss me, Gavin Kessler. I'll warm you up."

"Sounds romantic, but let's get to the car first, turn the heat on, and then get to that part."

She smiled. "You really don't like the cold, huh?"

By the time she finished her sentence I already had her and her dress safe in the car. I carefully walked to my side, probably looking somewhat like a penguin because I did not want to fall again and end up with more wet, cold slop on my pants.

I turned on the car. Ella's dress flew to the backseat. Her lips landed on mine. The local indie station played a folk song as I let her kiss warm me. Better than hot chocolate. Hands down.

She stopped kissing me. Looked at the radio. Back to me.

"Did you hear that?" she said.

"Hear what?"

"That news snippet. I think they said Mwenye."

I tugged on her collar. "About that kiss...."

She sat in her seat, eyes turned serious. "I think they just said Mwenye is in jail for murder."

Chapter Six

We parked around the block from Tylissa's house. She told us to climb the fence out back so the reporters wouldn't catch us. Last thing I wanted was to be on television with Harold Kessler roaming Pennsylvania, so I obliged. Albeit a nervous wreck. I'm an artist, not a sporty guy. I'm not ripped and I can't throw a football to save my life. Climbing six-foot fences did not appeal to me. Especially with freezing rain blowing in my face.

But all for the sake of love, I did it.

We climbed over and dropped to the ground. I'm not gonna lie, my ankle seared with pain like you wouldn't believe. I limped after Ella and followed her inside the back door.

Tylissa greeted us, face swollen, eyes red. I sat on the ground by the door, pulled one shoe off, and unlaced and slowly lifted the other. I wiggled a toe and jerked. Okay, so I'm a wimp. I get that. Most women want the big hero with a six-pack to lift them up and carry them into a passionate embrace. Then there's me. Wincing on the floor over what I hoped to be a sprained ankle and not a broken one.

Ella and Tylissa sat at the kitchen table completely oblivious of me. I hopped over and took a seat. Ella noticed. I motioned for her to sit down and worry about Tylissa instead. She hesitated, then tuned back in to her friend.

"I know he didn't do it," she said, anger hiding behind her clenched teeth. Her shoulders loosened, fell a few inches. "But he won't say that."

"I don't understand," Ella said.

"I wish I could tell you."

"Why can't you?"

"He won't let me."

Ella rubbed her chin and looked across the table toward me. I shrugged. She urged me to speak. I shrugged again, then mouthed, "What do I say?"

She shrugged. I shook my head and laughed inside.

"Tylissa," I said. "I've met Mwenye a few times now. I have no doubt that he's innocent, but why can't you tell others? If you know why or how this happened, you need to speak up. This could mean life or death for him. On the news they said they are considering death penalty because of the gruesome nature of the crime."

She wiped a tear from her face, and another, and another.

"I know you don't want that for him. If you can prove his innocence then you need to."

"I can't." Her sobs shook her body until she collapsed on the floor.

Almost immediately a baby cry echoed down the stairs. Ella jogged up the steps and out of sight, leaving me with the heartbroken woman curled up on the kitchen tile. I sat there, helpless, waiting for her to stop crying or for Ella to come downstairs. Didn't know what to do.

Ella walked back into the room, babyless, and sat on her knees next to Tylissa. No words. Just rubbed her back and waited.

The baby cried again.

Ella stood. "Could you come with me a second?"

She led me upstairs to a bedroom. "Make yourself at home in this room. I'm going to sleep with the baby and get Tylissa into her bed."

"This is crazy, Ella. You do realize that this is the worst school shooting in our history? It's one thing to walk into a high school, but to kill a bunch of students in a school for disabled children is quite a few clicks worse. And it wasn't a few kids either. According to the news seventy-something kids were reported dead on the scene and forty-one were seriously injured."

She nodded. "I can't believe it. Mwenye has such a sweet spirit."

"How did they get him? And why would he admit he's guilty if he's not? This isn't a game. He'll be on death row before we are married."

"I don't know. Maybe that's the media's spin on it. Let's wait until tomorrow."

I peeked out the window. Lights and cameras all over the place. Still.

Ella walked to the baby's room, then turned and came back to me.

"Almost forgot." She kissed me. "Goodnight."

"Night, love."

She walked away and said over her shoulder, "Ankle okay?"

I looked down. Forgot. "I guess it was just one of those weird ankle twist things."

I HELPED TYLISSA FIND AN ATTORNEY AS ELLA MADE FRIED eggs over English muffins, topped with tomatoes, fresh basil, and balsamic vinaigrette, with a side of her amazing crispy potatoes and onions. Steam hovered as she set three plates on the kitchen table and sat down with us.

"Will I be able to afford this?" Tylissa asked, switching her baby from one hip to the other and picking up her fork.

"It is expensive, but this is your husband's life," I said.

She caught a single tear in her sleeve. "But he will plead guilty." Her head shook and more tears dropped. "We were upstairs when they busted the door in. Just about to go to bed. I thought it was a robber. He pulled my face to his, kissed me, and told me to get a public defender, not an attorney, and let him do what he needed to do. I didn't even know what a public defender was. None of it made sense. Ten minutes after they took him I held the baby in the bedroom. I couldn't cry. I couldn't feel anything. I honestly had no idea what had happened until I started processing his last words to me."

"Can you explain to us what happened?" I said, taking a bite of Ella's deliciousness.

She put her pinky in her daughter's mouth and tried to catch her breath. "He made me promise I'd never tell anyone."

"But he will probably end up on death row."

"I know," she said. "I've known this for a long time."

"And you're okay with it?"

Her breathing slowed. "I promised."

Well, I couldn't have understood Tylissa if I tried, so I stopped trying and just listened, completely baffled as to why and how someone would allow their spouse to accept a guilty verdict in a terrible crime they didn't commit. Promises or not, I couldn't bear to watch someone I love die for something they didn't do. Maybe Tylissa valued faithfulness more than life. Or maybe Mwenye valued faithfulness more than his own life and that's why she couldn't break her promise to him. I wanted to understand. No matter how much my brain cells pondered various scenarios, I couldn't understand. Just couldn't.

Chapter Seven

April washed away the last of the March snow when my resume was turned down for the seventeenth time. I applied everywhere I could think of and wondered why I spent so much time and money in college for a degree that couldn't guarantee me a job to pay off the loans.

Ella tapped my shoulder as I drove over the bridge from Jersey to Philly. We spent the morning watching the sunrise on the ocean. Ella loved to drive to the beach for no reason. She called me at 3am and said, "Let's go." So I went. It happened five times since the day we met. She loved it and so did I.

She propped her feet up on the dashboard. "What are you thinking?"

"Nothing," I said. Instinct. "I mean, I don't know. I get spaced out with these windshield wipers. I was just thinking about money. School. Lack of jobs. We just bought a house and I have a savings account that is vanishing by the second. I need to find something quick."

"You will. And so will I." She looked over the bridge at the waves. "There's something I haven't told anyone."

"About the accident?"

"How'd you know?"

"Figured you'd be thinking about it. You always bring it up when we cross this bridge, but my question is ... if you can now play violin again, what's the big deal? Plus, if you wouldn't have missed that flight who knows if we would've ever met."

"Yeah, but there's something I don't tell anyone. I didn't want people feeling sorry for me or thinking I'm a horrible person."

"I can relate."

"I know, which is why I am going to tell you something if you promise to let me read the second letter when we get there."

"Deal."

She led me down random roads by pointing and repeating, "Oh, oh. I think it was that road back there. Sorry." When you're used to driving solo your entire life it gets weird when you share the road with another person. You see things you never saw before when you drive down the same tired roads. Suddenly things look new and different. That's the beauty of letting someone else drive. You look at life instead of road signs. So I didn't mind her sloppy directions. I enjoyed seeing her live.

We pulled into a graveyard. She got out of the car, rain boots hitting the rocky path. I loved the sound of shoes on gravel. I crunched my way over to her and put an umbrella over us. She led me down a hill and to a tree, where a lonely gravestone sat, although the teddy bears and flowers probably kept it company.

I read the name. Didn't ring a bell. Ella knelt down and kissed the earth. "I'm so sorry, Parker."

She pulled me down to sit with her, beside the etched stone.

"This is Parker," she said. "And he would be 13 years old today if I hadn't killed him."

"Don't be so hard on yourself. It was an accident."

"It wasn't, Gavin." She pulled a letter from her purse and placed it on the stone. "I'm not the only weirdo who carries letters." She smiled, moving the letter to a teddy bear's arms. "I've come to terms with it, but it's true. If I would've been paying attention and not speeding, I wouldn't have crossed the line. We can say it's an accident all we want, but it was something I could've easily prevented."

Rain pelted the top of the umbrella above our heads. She stared at the stone as I reached into my pocket and slid the envelope onto my lap. "This one is hard for me to read again."

She turned. "I love you."

I handed her the letter and watched her unfold the college-ruled paper between us. Rain dropped off the umbrella, wetting my shaking hand as she started to read.

Down from the Clouds

Dearest Gavin,

My dear boy, please know that I understand why you can't see me or talk to me right now. I don't take it personal and I will die knowing that you loved me too much to say goodbye, but you're avoidance of reality isn't going to change reality. I'm dying. One day you'll need to start accepting reality instead of trying to paint it into something fantastical. Sometimes life is fantastical, and other times you have to find fantastic inside of the boring parts and yes, even the pain.

If you can't learn to find joy regardless of your circumstances, you won't keep joy. You've gotta find it in the things that don't change, the things that live inside of you.

Heck, I'm old and my hand hurts. I don't know what I'm saying, but I do know this: you will find her one day and when you do you will have to stop hiding. I hope that by the time you find her you learn this. It's better to walk right up and hug pain because you love a person, then to run from it and never truly love.

I am still here, hanging on. I had to write this letter over three days, but I needed it to be my own hand writing it, not someone else's. They are amazed here at how much I can still think and do so close to my death. So weird, Gavin, to come face-to-face with death like this. Sometimes I sit here by myself and just stare at it. I don't know whether to laugh or to cry.

Still hoping for you to walk through that door any minute. I don't think I can hang on too much longer.

Pop

SILENCE ENFOLDED US AS WE DROVE HOME. NO MUSIC. NO cell phones. No conversation. Just wipers screeching, rain tapping the car

53

roof, and thunder rolling through the treetops as headlights swished by.

"You know what?" Ella said as we walked inside the house.

"What?" I shut the door and sat down on the couch.

"I learned something today."

"Enlighten me."

She sat down beside me, passion in her voice. "Sarah and I once talked about this, and I understand it a little more right now. Every day we're given a choice. To live or to die. I think it's a choice in everything. It's always about life or death. I can choose to love or choose to hate. Love is life, and hate is death."

"Whoa, whoa, hold on a second." I straightened my posture. "I didn't study philosophy in school."

She rolled her eyes. "I know you know what I'm saying."

I slapped her thigh with the back of my hand. "Go on. I'm sorry."

"So there's this choice. I was looking at his grave tonight, wondering why I couldn't move on. I realized why. Because I let Parker die. Do you see what I'm saying? If he lives on in my thoughts and memories, if I live for him, then it's like a part of him is still alive. I can keep him alive."

"I remember saying that to Heidi."

"And same with your grandfather. Only, I think sometimes we need to be the one to die. Like Matt with Lydia. Like all of us, really. We have to kill our own fears in order to find a way to love others."

Her face glowed, like she had unearthed a hidden treasure worth more than anything in the world.

"What happens when it's your own fear that kills you?" I said. "And then you're just dead, waiting for something to bring you back to life, but even the most beautiful thing in the world, the thing you thought you always wanted, doesn't resurrect you? What if you're just a mess underneath it all? So much that if you were an open book like so many pride themselves on being, people would stop reading after two seconds."

Her hand warmed the back of my neck. "I will never stop reading this story. Remember something, Gavin. This isn't your book anymore. It's ours."

Chapter Eight

Maybe it was wrong, but I couldn't help it. Not like anyone else should've been reading her letter anyway. And if they were curious, they would've picked it up and read it. There's no doubt about it. But I couldn't bring myself to open it. So I stuffed it in my pocket along with the unopened one from Pop.

My phone vibrated in my other pocket. I took it out and hit the button. "Hey, Matt. How's married life?"

"It's better and the same all at once." Wind distorted his voice. "Hey, I'm on my way to Heidi's house. Her baby had to go in for some kind of tests and Patrick says she's a mess."

"What happened? Is it serious?"

"He didn't say. Something to do with x-rays and amputation."

"Oh." I didn't pretend that it made sense to me. "What do you need me to do?"

"Patrick invited a few of us over tonight just to lift her spirits a little. Want to come?"

"I guess. Nothing better to do except count my dwindling savings account."

"Still no job?"

"Nothing."

"Where's Ella?"

"She's with Sarah. I'll ask her if they want to come too."

"You guys still living separately?"

"Yep."

"Why won't she just move in? The wedding is only a few months away."

"It's a year away. She wants it to be old-fashioned. She's obsessed with the regency era and everything up until about 1930. She thinks it all went downhill after that."

"And you agree?"

"Not really."

"So why do you go along with it?"

"Why do you think?"

"Alright. Well, see ya in a few then?"

"Yeah. I'll leave now."

I called Ella. Sarah said she'd love to come and Ella, of course, agreed. Nothing she enjoyed more than loving on people who needed it. By the time I parked outside Ella and Sarah were knocking on the door.

I turned off the car and walked to the porch. Ella wrapped her arms around my neck and stood on her toes. I loved when she did that.

"Alright you two," Sarah said. "I want a hug too. It's been months since I've seen you, Gavin."

"I know. How've you been? Obviously photography does much better than painting right now. I saw your website. Looks great."

"Thank you. I've been trying to focus more on engagement and wedding photography."

"Yeah," Ella said. "When will you be engaged? I still can't believe you won't bring James around for us to meet him."

"Actually, he's coming tonight. I was supposed to meet him after we finished looking at bridesmaids dresses, but since I'm here I thought he could be too."

"Interesting." Ella smiled and rubbed her hands together. Such a mischievous little Cupid. She loved relationships. I sometimes wondered why she didn't become a wedding planner. Would've been an ideal job for her.

My phone rang. I didn't recognize the number. When I went to ignore the call I accidentally picked up. I motioned for Ella and Sarah to go in while I took the call.

"Gavin?" The voice said. "Is that you?"

I tried to register the man's voice. Brain cells pulled up blank cards. "Who is this?"

"Please don't hang up."

"What is your name?"

"This is yo—I mean, this is Harold K-K-Kessler. Please do—"

I hung up and immediately accessed my cellular account via my iPhone to block his number. Call me unforgiving and cold all you want, but until you go through something like that yourself you can't judge my actions. That's the thing with life, isn't it? We spend our days judging everyone else when we don't know the entire story. And someone else is probably judging us just the same. I walked into Heidi's house with Eminem's *Beautiful* song playing in my head. I never liked rap. Growing up I was into grunge and lately I'd been on a jazz kick. No idea why. Maybe from the Cosby reruns I watched. Rap and I weren't friends, save the occasional Tupac. Eminem never made sense to me, until he wrote *Beautiful*. It's almost like he climbed inside my head when he wrote that.

I sat next to Ella. Yes, on the floor against the wall. Patrick, Heidi, and her baby were on the love-seat. Patrick held the baby. Matt, Lydia, and Sarah sat on the other couch.

The doorbell rang.

"I'll get it." Sarah jumped.

"What's the baby's name?" I whispered to Ella.

"Riley."

"And what's the deal with Heidi and Patrick? Are they together now?"

"They say they aren't, but I think the only people they are fooling are themselves."

Sarah cut in and I forgot what I wanted to say. She introduced her boyfriend, James. Ella and I stood and shook his hand and his little sister's hand.

"And what's your name?" Ella said to the young girl.

"Abigail," she said. "But they can call me Abby, right Daddy?"

"Of course," he said.

I looked at Ella. Eyebrows raised, she tried her best to hide her feelings, but whether she wanted them on her face or not they were there.

I pulled Ella away. Sarah could thank me later. In the kitchen, I held her hand and kissed it. "I know this is not what you wanted for Sarah, but if it's what she wants you need to let it happen. She probably hid this from you for so long knowing that you'd react this way."

Ella's eyes darted around the kitchen. "I can't believe this."

"Everyone's love story has it's own words, it's own feel. You can't write every single story the same way. Life would be boring that way."

"Okay." She wiggled her fingers and exhaled. "Why does this bother me so much?"

"Maybe you aren't settled enough in your own decisions?"

"What is that supposed to mean, Gavin? You know how I feel about you."

"I know. Trust me, I know that. I just mean . . . sometimes we fear other people making decisions we wouldn't make because it blows wind on our dreams. If our dreams are shaky, the wind blows it over. If our dreams are solid, the wind can turn into a tornado and it wouldn't matter."

"What do you think I'm dreaming about that isn't solid?"

"All I'm saying is maybe you need to worry about making your own dreams solid and if some wind blows this way you won't have to defend yourself or offend others. You can just live your own life and be content."

"I can't think clearly right now to know if what you're saying makes any sense at all, but one thing I do know is that I'm not upset because of wind blowing on my dreams. I'm upset because my dream came true and my best friend is settling."

Patrick walked in. "Hey, when's the big day for you guys?"

Ella faked a smile as I pulled her into me. Her shoulder fit right underneath my arm. Perfect.

"It's in the beginning of December. We wanted a simple winter wedding. Nothing elaborate."

"Nothing like Matt and Lydia's?"

"No. Not at all. They started out trying to go the simple route, but never quite made it. We are inviting less than fifty people. Light reception after, no sit-down meals. Anyway, how's Heidi and Riley? I don't understand what happened."

Patrick lifted a glass from the cabinet behind us. "You guys want something to drink?"

"No, thanks."

"Riley has fibular hemimelia. Basically one of the bones in her leg didn't form right in the womb, and now one leg is shorter than the other."

"What was upsetting Heidi today?"

"She was given two choices today. One, they amputate Riley's leg and treat her with prosthetics."

Ella perked up. "Wow. I didn't realize."

"Or two, they correct the bone and over time Riley would need approximately five lengthening surgeries. They attach a thing to her leg and we would have to turn the pins each day to lengthen the bone. Her case is considered a severe difference in lengths. Most people in our shoes amputate."

I couldn't help but notice his use of "we" as he referred to Heidi and himself. I have no doubt Ella noticed too.

"What's Heidi going to do, then?" Ella said.

"She wants to lengthen and if Riley decides on her own at some point to amputate then she will support it."

I shook my head. "What a hard decision."

ELLA PRETENDED TO BE HAPPY FOR SARAH THE REST OF THE night. Even played tic-tac-toe with Abby. I knew as soon as we got into the car she'd explode, but we drove off and she didn't speak. We got home, made small talk, grabbed a can of paint and some brushes, and started painting our soon-to-be bedroom an antique green.

"I think you're right." She looked at her engagement ring, making sure it didn't have paint on it. "But I think you need to start taking advice, too."

I nodded. Harold's voice hurting my head. What advice would I give myself if I weren't me?

"Gavin."

I am not the crying type. I don't take pride in it either. I'm not a macho man. My tears dried up when I was in elementary school and they only returned for two brief moments. One, when I saw Ella on the news and realized she was waiting for me too. And two, when I received the last letter from Pop four days after he died.

My well dried up. Maybe that's why no one could pull any water out. I had nothing left. And I'd give anything to cry again. Really cry. Get this feeling out of me and wash it away in the bathtub.

"Are you okay?" Ella reached for my shoulder. "You seem out of it."

"Harold Kessler called."

"And?"

"I hung up on him."

My iPod shuffled. I turned up the music. Fleetwood Mac. *The Chain*. We listened. That would be normal, except that Ella and I never listened to that song. We always sang when it came on.

I turned it down. "What are you thinking?"

She hesitated.

"What advice would you give me?"

"I don't know anymore. We aren't even married yet and everything around us is falling apart. It's making me doubt everything I once believed."

"What are you doubting?"

"My own definition of love. Do soul-mates exist? And if they do, do you remarry when they die? What about people who abuse you or leave you? Do you let them back into your heart? This relationship between you and me. What is it? What are we?" She inhaled. Bit her lip. "What is love, Gavin?"

Chapter Nine

We allowed Ella's question to hover in the air between us for weeks. Neither of us knew the answer. Or at least knew how to answer it. Instead, we occupied ourselves with a new business venture. All the credit goes to Ella. My little business woman. We decided to call it "Studio K." I didn't like the name. At all. But she insisted. We'd teach ages one to twelve how to paint, draw, mold, sculpt, build, and also offer piano, guitar, bass, drums, violin, cello, flute, and voice lessons. Yes, between the two of us we knew how to do every one of those things.

According to the organization queen, we'd start out with lessons in our basement since it had a separate entrance and good setup for sound and mess. Then we'd move to a studio in the city after we saved enough money. Not in a million years did I imagine this working out, but I humored her. I loved her excitement. In the few short months that I spent with her I could already see her intense drive to devote herself one-hundred percent to something or not at all. I loved seeing her put herself into these things, but it worried me a little. I saw that personality get burned out more times than I can count. Sitting on the sidelines of life gives you a lot of time to think about what you don't want to do if you ever decide to play. And spending life as a pendulum wasn't something I wanted to do. Any second those pendulums could fly right off into some oblivion. Balance, when savored with passion, can do a soul good.

I let Ella run with the business plans and boy did she run.

"You sure you don't need my help?" I yelled down the basement steps.

"I don't need it." Her voice echoed back. "But I always want you near me."

"Patrick wanted to meet up with Matt and I tonight. Should I go?"

"If you come and kiss me first."

WE FINISHED OUR DESSERT IN THE DIMLY LIT RESTAURANT. Matt asked the waiter for another water. Patrick and I did the same.

"So," Matt said. I knew what would come next.

"You wanna know if Heidi and I are together?" Apparently Patrick knew too.

Matt nodded and shrugged. Then sipped his water as he motioned for Patrick to tell us. I swear Matt had the mind of a woman sometimes. Maybe even most times. He loved relationship details. I feel uncomfortable asking people what kind of underwear they buy and how many times they have sex a year. Not Matt.

"We're just friends." He cleared his throat. "Best friends. But just friends."

I smiled. "Come on. Are you trying to make yourself believe that?"

"We see the way you look at each other." Matt slipped the waiter his credit card. I knew he'd try to pay for the entire meal. He always did.

"I'm not gonna lie. I fell in love with her. She knows it, but she wanted to stay committed to Andy and she's trying to stick to it." He sighed. "I don't know how or why we met, but if anything, I'm going to be there for her until the day one of us dies."

"What are the chances?" I imagined Ella's face the first night I finally kissed her.

"The chances of what?"

"Of you losing your wife and Heidi losing her husband and you both falling in love when you both vowed not to?"

"I don't know. What are the chances?"

"Tell me this," Matt said. "What was your relationship like with your wife?"

"Honestly?" He rubbed his facial hair, repositioned himself, and looked down. "It was hard."

"Because she was dying?"

"No, because she wanted to die." He exhaled. "I gave my life to that girl. Just couldn't fix her. I did love her though. Loved her with every ounce in me."

I leaned forward. "What were you trying to fix?"

"She had a lot of trauma from her past. I wanted to help her heal, but it's almost as though she didn't want to heal. She loved me. And I promised my life to her. But we were never lovers."

"You mean you never had sex? Not even once?"

"Yes." Patrick sipped his water until only ice cubes were left.

"Why?"

"She was raped by her father as a child. She never wanted me to touch her. Sometimes I'd reach for her hand and she'd flinch." He shook his head as though the very memories would fall to the ground and disappear if he shook hard enough.

"So it was like being married to your best friend, but no romance?" I said.

"We had romance. Just not in your typical Ella Rhodes way."

I smiled. "Understatement."

"Gavin has a lot to live up to," Matt said.

I laughed. "I'd dress in a Prince Charming outfit and parade around in a horse drawn carriage if she asked me to." Once our laughter died down I looked at Patrick. "Can I ask you something?"

He nodded.

"If you didn't have sex or touch, and you didn't feel loved in return, how did you love her so much?" I held up my hand. "Wait. I know that sounds bad. I don't mean it like that. I guess what I'm asking is, how would you define the love that you guys had?"

Patrick tilted his head and squinted, absorbed in memories. Matt crunched an ice cube as we waited for him to answer.

"Well," he said. "I'm not sure I can explain what we had."

"Why did you marry her?"

"Sometimes things just don't make sense to the world. I think love is one of those things. The more we try to think about it and define it, the more we distort it with ourselves. Our own opinions of love. But for us, I don't know, we were connected. We didn't have much in common. We argued a lot. I tried to fix her and she resented me for it, thinking I didn't love her for who she was. But I loved her for who she was. She just didn't know herself."

"How is it different with Heidi?" Matt said.

"Heidi." He smiled. "She is strong. There's something mysterious about her, but in a healthy way. I can't explain it. Does that make sense? She has been through a lot, but she handles it well. She's different than my wife was. She's happier. She has her down moments, but she genuinely wants to be better. To grow."

"No, I mean, how do your feelings for her differ?"

He thought for a minute, then said, "Heidi and I have a chemistry I never had with Emily. I tried to make myself believe we did. I sent her flowers, love letters, practically devoted every waking moment to her. But she never returned the love. I often wonder if it took me so long to get out of bed after she died because I had spent those years of my life at her feet. I forgot there was life outside of her." He closed his eyes and took a breath. "Anyway, Heidi felt the same way. Her and Andy had a great relationship, but it never had a chance to grow deeper. It was still new and fresh. A young romance that died too soon. That changes a person though. Makes them look at life differently. I think what Heidi and I have is something deeper. It's almost like falling in love backwards. Starting deeper and maybe one day the romance and excitement will set in. Or maybe we will be friends for life. Nothing more."

"Wow." Matt looked around the room. "And all this time time I thought Gavin and I were the only guys like this."

"Like what?" I said.

"Guys who aren't into one night stands and really want to love a woman the way they deserve. That's why it took me so long to commit to Lydia. She's beyond perfect, and she deserved the best. Until I knew I could give her what she deserved, genuinely, I couldn't do ask her to marry me."

"Yes," I said. "There's a shortage of men who don't think with either of their heads as much as they think with this." I patted my chest. "You know what other guys would call us, right?"

Patrick laughed. "A choice five letter word that begins with a P and ends with a Y?"

Chapter Ten

I walked through the door. So eager to see Ella. A few hours away from her tortured me. I found her in the kitchen. Tired eyes. Hair clinging to her cheeks.

She saw me. An envelope fell from her hand. Landed by my foot.

"How could you?" She picked up another envelope from the counter. "I didn't open yours." She flung it at my chest. "If you would've asked I would've read it to you. Unlike you, I have nothing to hide."

Arms at my sides, dangling there like broken limbs, I tried to speak.

"Say something. Please. I'm trying to deal with all of these secrets you have. I really am. I'm an open book and the love of my life won't let me get past chapter four." Her volume increased. "I know I have my own issues, but please. You are a grown man, Gavin. Stop acting like a child."

I couldn't move. Couldn't speak. Not even to tell her that I hadn't read her letter. That I loved her. That I was sorry. That I wanted to open up to her, but didn't know where to start.

She closed her eyes. Tilted her head back. "Say something, Gavin. Anything."

I didn't want to be irritated with her. I really didn't, but her words didn't help. "I don't think I'm acting like a child." I should've walked away. Or at least kept my mouth shut.

"That's all you have to say? It's not even that you took the letter. I'll share anything with you. It's that you didn't tell me." She inhaled and looked at me. Made eye contact for the first time I walked in. "I don't like secrets. I want to know you."

I bent down and picked the envelope up. Turned it over. Addressed to me. Probably the last letter he ever wrote.

Ella kneeled beside me. "I know this is hard for you."

"It's not an excuse."

"I'm sorry." She touched my hand. "I'm just overwhelmed. I want to be your best friend. You have to open up to me."

"No," I said. "Don't apologize. It's my fault. I'm sorry. Sorry for everything. I know I'm not the knight in shining armor you were hoping for."

She pulled a hair off my shoulder. "Your armor is a little rusty, but with a little work it will look good as new. Not like this princess is so great either."

"You are to me."

She smiled and pressed her forehead into my shoulder. I put my arm around her and pulled her into my chest. We held each other on the kitchen floor.

"I still think you're acting like a child though." She kissed my cheek. "Can you please read the letter and move on from this? I doubt your grandfather wanted you to sit around and dwell on it."

"That's exactly what I'm afraid of."

"What?"

"Moving on. Writing 'the end' and forgetting the story."

My phone rang.

"You can pick it up," she said.

"You know how I feel about answering the phone when I'm with you."

"You'll have to get used to it sometime. Now that we are going to be working together you'll be around me all the time."

I looked at the number. Didn't recognize it. "It's probably Harold Kessler. He's been calling from random numbers and leaving messages."

"What do the messages say?"

"Don't know."

"You don't listen to them?"

I rubbed my head.

"Let me listen."

"I really d—"

"Don't make me break out the indian burn." She laughed. "Seriously, let me listen."

I handed her the phone. Too tired to argue my way out of it. She pressed a few buttons and held the phone to her ear. I could hear. All five messages she listened to. Same thing. "Gavin, please call me. I just want to talk to you once and I'll leave you alone after that."

Ella slid the phone into my hand. "Call him."

"And say what?"

"Whatever you want." She kissed my fingers. "I will be here for you. It's not that bad. Just a phone call is all he wants from you."

I stood. Walked to the couch and took off my shoes. "Can I read the letter instead?"

She propped her head up with some pillows and hid her feet under my legs. "Sure."

"And if I read this letter do you promise not to ask me to talk to that man?"

She held up her pinky. I linked it with mine.

The letter looked aged. Hadn't been a year since he mailed it, but the yellowed envelope and frayed edges said otherwise. I tore a corner off and slid my finger inside. Ella's eyes, on me, were bright now that the tears subsided. I tried to smile.

Holding my breath, I ripped open the top and pulled the letter out. Only one sheet of paper. I expected a novel for his last words. Not a paragraph.

Ella wiggled her feet under my body. "Open it."

I obeyed. Blue ink formed a single paragraph. My eyes glazed over at the first three words. Crying scared me. Not because I wanted to pretend to be all tough and never get hurt. I'm not a fan of the "suck it up" mentality. Tears scared me because I held so much inside. For decades. Releasing a few tears, I worried, would break the dam. So I blinked away the droplets on my eyes and read aloud so Ella could hear.

Dearest Gavin,

I forgive you. Please don't let it eat at you for the rest of your life. Live. If not for yourself, do it for me. That's the one last thing I ask of you. Live. Please accept that I don't hold this against you. I only have one request of you. Go to the old apple tree we used to swing on. I buried a box there before my health declined. I had a feeling you'd

avoid my death, so I prepared something for you. Go there as soon as
you can and do everything exactly as I have written. Please.
  Till then,
  Pop

Chapter Eleven

O
f course Ella insisted on driving to the apple tree at the crack of dawn. I knew she would. I begged her to stay the night with me, but she also insisted on her Jane Austen policy. And because I loved her more than anything on the planet, I conceded to both.

We let the windows down as we drove to Lancaster County. Spring air revived us, along with Third Eye Blind and Michael Jackson. As I twisted and turned down country roads, we sang along and held hands. When Meatloaf came on we sang as loud as possible. Ella climbed onto her seat and stuck her head out of the sunroof. Hands outstretched, face toward the sky, hair tossed in a million directions, she inspired me. Inspired me in more ways than I can express.

Finally, we pulled up to the place Pop and I had parked so many times before. I parked under an oak tree and opened Ella's door.

"This is beautiful." She placed her hand over her eyes and looked around. "How did you find this?"

"Pop owns this land. His house was right over there." I pointed across the hills to a large, secluded colonial house with ivy climbing the sides. "That's where I grew up."

"He owns all of this?"

I breathed in the lilac scent. Then closed my eyes and imagined Pop putting me on his shoulders and running at full speed. We'd both tumble and laugh as we rolled down the hill. He couldn't do it once he hit eighty-five, after his heart attack. So we walked down together. His arm linked with mine. Took us forty-minutes to get to the same apple tree that we ran to in five.

I didn't mind. Loved every second with him. Just like I did with my

Ella.

She walked to the blooming lilac. "I love this smell."

"Pick some off," I said, walking toward her.

"I couldn't." She leaned in and inhaled. "I always feel bad breaking branches. Look at it." She smiled. "So full of life and beauty. If I cut some off it will smell good for a few hours, but lose all of its life."

I moved the hair out of her face and ran my fingers along her cheek. I stopped at her chin and pulled it to mine. "I love you more than I did yesterday."

She closed her eyes. I kissed her. And stopped. And kissed her again.

Ten minutes later we raced down the hill. Like kids again. She pulled her skirt up as we crossed a small stream, then walked up the other side.

When we reached the top of the hill, Ella gasped and covered her mouth. Eyes darting around. Taking it in. She looked at me and laughed. "I can't believe you grew up here. This is amazing. It's like the Secret Garden meets Huckleberry Finn."

I laughed. "The apple tree is over there."

"Wow. I thought apple trees were done blooming by May?"

"It's a Rome Beauty apple tree. Pop planted it for my grandmother when they moved here. She loved the pink and white flowers that came every year around this time, but she hated the apples."

Ella smiled and walked toward the tree. "What's wrong with the apples?"

"They're okay. Better for baking pies. Pop and I weren't so good at that, so we let the animals eat the fruit and gave some away to the neighbors. Or he'd let me set up a stand on the side of the road and sell some fruit. Never made much, but it was fun."

"I love this place, Gavin." She smelled a flower from the apple tree. "Who owns it now?"

"No idea. Never saw his will, if he has one. Don't know how much he owed on the place. I wouldn't want to live here though. I want a new life with you."

She sat on the tire swing and lifted her feet. "So little Gavin sat on this swing?"

I walked behind her and gave her a push. "He did."

My hands shook. Beads of sweat dripped down my neck when I saw the mound of dirt next to the tree, underneath the carvings I made as a kid.

Ella hopped off the swing. "Ready?"

"I forgot a shovel."

"Have no fear." She shook her purse and pulled out a small shovel. "I come prepared."

"You are too much."

"It's the fallout from my type A organization skills. Hoping to get rid of that a bit and be normal again."

I took the shovel and sunk it into the earth, trying not to think too much about what I would discover.

Ella sat on her knees next to me. The shovel hit something hard. I dug around and pulled out a box. Plain wood. About the size of a ruler on both sides and three inches deep.

"It's locked," she said.

I wiped the dirt off the top and flipped the box upside down.

She read aloud.

Wait until you find her, because I know you will. When you do, take this box and find the key. My will is inside and it's the only copy. And there's something else that's important for you to read. You need to find the key. First clue: the road where they found you when your dad left.

I stood. Without the shovel. Or the box. "This is ridiculous. What kind of game is this? I don't care about the will. I want nothing. He gave me plenty and I gave him nothing. I can't take more."

Ella sat in the dirt, box in her hands, smile on her face. "This is beautiful."

"It's not. It's manipulative. I'm not going back to that road. I've spent my life avoiding it."

"That's exactly why this is so beautiful."

"Why?"

She stood in front of me, eyes sparkling as specks of sunlight danced on her face. "Because he knows you better than anyone ever did. He knew you wouldn't come to him when he died, so he did this. Maybe it's a way for you to relive your memories with him."

"I relive them all the time."

"Let go, Gavin. Just let go."

"Of what?"

"Of all that bitterness. Just let it go and let's have fun with this."

HE PROBABLY TOLD ME TO WAIT UNTIL I FOUND HER BECAUSE he knew she'd make sure I followed the directions until I found the key. Pop never lacked brains. Wisest person I'd ever known. Quiet, soft-spoken, and barely said a word unless necessary. He knew when to speak and when he did everyone listened. Except my dad.

Didn't take long for us to find the road. Only a minute from Pop's house. I asked him to tell me the story once when I was nine years old and I remembered every detail since. When Ella asked, I told her exactly what I remembered, "Dad put my car seat underneath a Japanese maple tree. Cops said the lady who lived in the house came out to water her flowers in the morning and saw the seat. I hadn't cried at all. Never even stirred. She thought I was dead and called the police. By the time they arrived I was in her arms, adjusting to the light around me. Pop knew the lady well. People called her Mama Jane. A widow since her husband died in World War II, she spent her days caring for everyone within a 5 mile radius. No exceptions. Pies, cookies, diapers, anything anyone needed at any time, somehow Mama Jane knew and took care of them. She'd leave anonymous bundles on the porch, but everyone knew it was her. Smelled just like her house. An unmistakeable blend of cinnamon and juniper."

I parked along the road and looked at the porch. Mama Jane died years ago. Pop and I went to the funeral along with hundreds of others. Everyone left little baskets on her grave, filled with flowers and notes, just like the baskets she left for so many of us.

Now, the porch lacked life. The garden should have been blooming by now, but the flowers died along with her.

"Does anyone live here?" Ella said.

"Not sure."

"Should we dig up their yard without asking?"

I turned the car off and walked up to the porch. Ella reached for my hand. Broken wood creaked under our feet. The screen door hung by one hinge. I peeked inside. Something moved. I opened the screen door and knocked.

A man stepped forward. Stained t-shirt and dirt-covered hands. The screen door fell toward Ella. She leaned into me.

"I'm sorry," she said, clinging to my arm.

"Ah, don't worry about it," the man said. "Needed a new one anyway."

"Wish you were as nice to me." A woman's voiced screamed from the house. Something crashed by the front door and shattered at our feet.

"Don't mind her. Woke up on the wrong side of the bed." He leaned in. The scent of whiskey on his breath. "She always does."

"Sorry to bother you, but my grandfather used to live near here. At the time a lady we called Mama Jane lived here." I pointed behind me. "He buried something under that tree for me to find and I was just wondering if it would be a problem for us to dig it up."

He spit across the porch. "No problem, man. Do what you need to do."

"Thank you," Ella said, peering behind him. "We'll make sure to clean it up."

He smiled and spit again, then closed the door. As we walked down the steps we heard more yelling and crashing. Ella tugged on my shirt and looked over her shoulder. "Should we do something?"

"None of our business."

"But maybe we were sent here for a reason."

"We were. And we're standing in front of it." I looked at the pile of dirt under the tree. "Got the shovel in your Mary Poppins bag?"

She lifted it out. I dug as she stared at the house. Never took her eyes off. I always believed her eyes were emerald for a reason. I called them emerald city eyes. Dark. Looked brown from a distance, but when you got close enough you'd see the most beautiful green staring back at you. Emerald City. The place where people realized their dreams were never far off to begin with. Hope. She never saw anyone as hopeless and she ached over the pain others felt.

I pulled a plastic bag out of the ground and looked up at Emerald City, then sang a line from my favorite Petty song, "You got a heart so big, it could crush this town."

"You sure we shouldn't do something?"

"What can we do?"

She knelt down and filled the dirt back in. "Let's come back tonight. When they're sleeping. We can buy some flowers and redo the garden. Maybe it will start to bring them back to life too."

"You got a heart so big, it could crush this town."

She patted the earth as she looked at the house. "It's no bigger than anyone else's."

We drove off as she opened the bag and read Pop's words.

Mama Jane lived for others because she had no one else. So everyone thought. But she did that long before Benjamin died. Go to her grave. I buried something under a tree. Stand at her grave. Then take 23 steps to the right. You'll see it.

"It's a good thing we're both unemployed."

She laughed. "We're not unemployed. We are starting our own business."

"No." I smiled. "We are driving around Pennsylvania digging up notes from my dead grandfather."

"You have to admit," she said. "It is kind of fun."

"Yeah."

"And doesn't a little part of you feel like he's alive again?"

"I wish."

We parked and walked to Mama Jane's grave. Covered in baskets and flowers.

"It's been years since I've been here." I looked to the right and counted twenty-three steps. Ella followed.

"I don't see anything," she said.

"I do." I knelt under the tree. "Shovel?"

"Does your grandfather have a thing for trees?"

I laughed. "Actually he does." I pulled out another bag and filled in the dirt. "He planted at least a hundred trees in his lifetime. He always used to say that trees were like people who didn't waste their life and truly lived."

She squinted her eyes and tilted her head. "How so?"

"That's what I said when he told me. He said because they were planted by someone else, needed lots of sun and water and attention in the beginning. If the wind or animals broke them early on they'd never make it, but if they were protected they would grow stronger. The stronger they grew, the less they'd break in a storm. And if they got to that point they'd live for a really long time, leaving their mark on tons of lives after that. They could never be uprooted, just a few dead branches broken here and there, but never uprooted."

"Wow."

"Know what I said when he told me that?"

"What?"

"I was eight at the time. I said, 'What if someone cuts it down for fire wood?'"

She laughed. "How profound of you."

"When I turned nine I woke up and rolled over in bed. Wrapped up in blue and white-striped paper was *The Giving Tree* by Shel Silverstein."

"I loved that story when I was a kid."

"Me too. Pop said he spent most of his life being the boy in the story, but I never thought so. I definitely considered him to be my tree. He always told me to live my life like the tree, not the boy. To be a giver and not a taker. Maybe that's one of the reasons I shove everything inside."

We sat in the car, a blanket of silence draped over us. Seconds turned into minutes.

Ella cleared her throat and wiped away the relaxed silence. "Sometimes giving means opening up and letting others know you. Sometimes the best thing you can give someone is yourself. The real you. All of you."

I held her face with both hands and leaned forward. Our lips met and lingered in place, no movement, just together. I pulled away, her breath still on my lips, and reached in the bag for the next note.

Remember, Gavin, Mama Jane was a giver. That's why so many people remembered her when she died, but the real amazing thing is that she never knew it. She didn't live her life to be remembered.

She didn't want fame or honor. All that time she thought she loved anonymously, but she didn't realize that true love can never be hidden. People always know when someone loves. No matter how much they try to hide their beauty, it's written all over the place. That's what I want for you, Gavin. That's what I want you to teach your children too. Be a giver. Not because you want something out of it. Because it's who you are. Next clue: The Giving Tree. I hope you still have the book. If not, you'll never find the next clue.

"Do you have it?" Ella asked.

"Somewhere."

"Where would it be?"

"Probably in a box in the basement. I have no idea. I didn't give it away though."

We kept the music off as we drove back to Philly. Just left the windows down and listened to life. My mind peeled back pages of dog-eared memories. Of everything Pop did for me. All the laughter and tears. The advice he gave me when people made fun of me at school. I loved him so much. I hoped he knew it. He gave me everything and I couldn't even bring myself to give him one last hug, to go to his funeral, to sit on the ole tree stump one last time.

Chapter Twelve

We found the journal as soon as we got home. In a box of books I hadn't unpacked since I came home from college. The last page had a short note in blue ink. *When you read this you'll know what it is. Go to the place where you learned how to really fight.* After that we drove to a local garden store and picked out two-hundred dollars worth of flowers and shrubs. I'm an art guy. You'd think I could've kept up with Ella, but I knew nothing about plants. She zoomed around with a huge smile on her face, dumping more and more on the cart by the minute. When we got back to the house I, once again, begged her to stay.

"Well, since we have to get up at three in the morning I will consider it."

"Consider it?" I pretended to cry.

"I'd have to sleep on the couch though." She shook her head. "No, no. What am I thinking? I want it to be right."

"What's so wrong with it? We're engaged. That's practically married. I'm not asking you to climb into bed with me, just to sleep under the same roof."

She raised her eyebrows. "I know it's weird. We don't live in the golden days anymore, but I wish I did. I love that they barely even saw each other alone until they were married. It's so romantic."

I sighed. "Let's get married tomorrow."

"Let's do this properly." She smiled. "I know it's ridiculous to everyone around us, but I want to be different. Every love story in the universe involves passionate sex before marriage and a live-in roommate. Or people with promise rings to God who do everything except sex and think they are justified. That's not romance to me. The other thing we forget is that most of these promise ring and passionate roommate marriages end up in divorce. Once they get bored or someone is unfaithful they go looking for a new playmate. I'm not interested in a playmate, Gavin. I'm interested in a soulmate. We will never be apart. Ever. No matter what. So don't make me start this on the wrong note. I want it to be right. To be romantic. And to be different. I want to beat the odds with you."

I pulled her close and kissed her, then tickled her until we both ended up on the floor in tears.

"I love you so much, Ella. I want it to be right too. I don't think beginning our life together on this note will change the future though. I think it's a choice every day. And no matter what, even if it means reliving a Jane Austen tale, I choose you. Over and over again, I'll choose you."

THE CLOCK IN MY CAR READ 3:21AM WHEN I PULLED UP IN front of Ella's apartment building, right next to the building Matt and I used to live in. Still couldn't believe she lived right there. I searched all over the place for her and she was right next to me.

She hopped in the car and shut the door. "Sarah thinks we're crazy."

"We are."

"But she likes it. She's been wanting me to live again. You've brought out the spontaneity I've been suppressing for so long."

I took her hand and accelerated. "If I start to doze off, slap my face."

"Seriously?"

I nodded. "I couldn't sleep. Kept thinking about Pop. His will."

"What about it?"

"I'm really worried he left the house to me. I'd feel horrible getting rid of it, but at the same time I can't live there."

"Why not?"

"Lots of reasons. Especially because Harold Kessler is bound to show up there. Probably already has."

"You need to face him sometime, Gavin."

"I don't need to, but I probably have to."

"Has he called anymore?"

"Yes. Different number every time. No idea how he's doing that."

"Maybe a pay phone?"

"I haven't seen a pay phone in years."

"Good point."

We talked as we drove. Flowers piled up in the backseat made it hard to see anything behind me. After hitting that dear I became a little paranoid in the car. Wasn't interested in dying soon, especially in a car wreck. An hour-and-a-half later we parked in front of Mama Jane's old house. Looked more like an abandoned house. Lights were out. Nothing but the sound of crickets to serenade us as we planted. Ella wanted to plant in the dark. No flashlights. If someone saw us they might stop us, and Ella wouldn't have that. She was on a mission to resurrect a marriage that was probably never alive in the first place. I didn't think the garden would help, but I didn't tell her that. There were times when I envied her idealism. Ugliness stared her right in the face and she always found something beautiful to say. At least most times. I loved that about her.

"Well." I rubbed my hands together. "Hope it looks okay when the sun comes up."

"We'll come back and check."

"Ready to go to the next place?"

We gathered our things and drove off. Only took ten minutes to get to the next place. The sky, still dark, didn't help. So for once I took advantage of technology and used the flashlight on my iPhone. Ella held the light while I dug a hole in the playground. Right under the sliding board. Couldn't believe they still had the same sliding board.

"What's the story with this place?" she said, sitting down.

I pulled out yet another plastic bag. Couldn't believe no one found these before I did. "My first fight. This was a playground Dad, I mean, Pop, let me come to alone. First summer I could ride my bike out of his sight, I came here. Didn't do much. I was too shy to make friends, but some kids from school started making fun of Pop. He talked with a little stutter. Nothing major, but there nonetheless. They started talking to me with a stutter and I hate to say it, but I punched the kid right in the face. Gave him a bloody nose, got on my bike, and rode like a bat out of hell."

"Thank you, Meatloaf."

"That was for you, darling. Nothing as Jane Austen-like as some epic

Meatloaf."

She laughed. "What's this note say?"

I unfolded it. *Salty shores and life guards galore.*

"The beach?"

"Don't get too excited." I stood and motioned for her to follow me back to the car. "It's just the community pool."

"Let's stay and swing together for a minute."

I stuffed the note in my pocket and sat on a swing. She sat next to me.

"You know," she said, legs out, head back. "When you proposed you said you thought of me all the time when you were a kid. I bet you sat on this swing and thought of me at some point."

I swung higher. "I did."

"What did you think?"

"I wondered who would swing higher and if I double dared you in a jumping contest who could land furthest away."

We laughed and swung as high as we could.

"In the count of three," I said. "One, two, three. Jump."

We jumped off and landed in the mulch. Ella about five inches further than me.

"Not fair," I said. "You cheated."

"No, I didn't." She fell back in laughter and pointed. "You are holding your ankle again."

"Don't make fun of me."

We laughed so hard we cried and probably toned our abs quite a bit. Eventually, I got my wish. She fell asleep under the moonlight. Head supported by my shoulder, tucked into my arm. I watched her sleep until the pink and orange sky painted her cheeks and woke her up. She rubbed her eyes and smiled.

I kissed her forehead. "Did Austen turn over in her grave?"

"You forget about Maryanne Dashwood. She would've done this. At least maybe."

"Which one is she again?"

"We'll watch it soon." She stood and brushed the mulch off. "Ready to go to the pool?"

"Yeah. Let's get there before anyone shows up."

Another car pulled into the parking lot as we got into the car. Ella's phone rang. She looked at me. "Tylissa. Should I answer?"

"Yes."

As she tried to calm Tylissa someone knocked on my window. I hit a button and watched the glass disappear.

"Sorry to b-b-bother you," the man said. "I'm looking f-f-for directions. You from around here?"

"Sort of."

"I need to get b-b-back to Route 30." He leaned in. "You look f-familiar. What's your name?"

"Gavin."

The man stepped back. "Kessler?"

"Who are you?"

He shook his head. Looked like he might cry. "You have your m-m-mother's eyes."

HONESTLY, WHAT ARE THE CHANCES? I SPENT MY ENTIRE LIFE searching for my bride when most boys wanted one night stands. Lived in the building next to hers, probably passed her a thousand times, even went into her coffee shop, asked to have my paintings sold there, and never saw her until I happened to turn on the news one night after a long day.

What are the chances?

And to spend my entire life trying to avoid the man I hoped would never come back unless the police found a remnant of his dead body from years ago, proving that he didn't leave me intentionally, only to have him knock on my car window to ask for directions?

Ella didn't believe in chances anymore. Since we met. She said she spent her entire life dreaming of the day "chances" would bring us together again, only to find out that every choice, whether it brought disaster or beauty, led her to the place she was meant to be. "The secret," she said. "Is waiting. Being patient and content where you are and hoping for what is yet to come."

So, maybe that explains why I pulled out of the parking lot and left him standing there, arms at his sides, squinting under his baseball hat, alone.

Maybe I didn't want to admit that perhaps that man, Harold Kessler, my long lost selfish father, came back into my life the same way Ella did. Not by chance. But because he was meant to.

That's the last thing I wanted to believe. The absolute last.

When we got to the pool Ella hung up with Tylissa and pulled my chin toward her. "I know who that was."

"How?"

"I heard him. I saw him. Gavin, you look just like him."

"I don't think so."

"Let's go back."

"No."

"Let's go back now, Gavin. I'm not kidding. He didn't look mean. If he had some kind of vendetta against you he would have followed us."

"I don't think he is trying to beat me up, Ella." I laughed. "I think he's trying to ask for forgiveness."

"What's so hard about that?"

"A person can't give something they don't have."

"Then don't give it to him, but at least see what he has to say. Tell him you can't forgive him. Be honest. You are his son. He's alive. There's a such thing as second chances."

"Oh yeah? What about Heidi and Patrick? Do you only believe in second chances when it's convenient for you?"

"Don't." She reached for my hand. "Don't do this to us. Our relationship deserves better. Don't let some anger and pain from your past build a wall between us."

"I can't see him."

She pulled the car handle. "Let's go find the next note. See what Pop has to say. You know I don't believe in chances anymore. Maybe this next note will tell you to turn back and face him."

I got out of the car. She knew me too well, better than I wanted to know myself. People thought of me as joyful, peaceful, optimistic, fun. Only Ella knew that I struggled just as much as the next person.

I pointed to the ground and Ella dug up the letter. I blamed the lack of sleep for my zapped energy, but seeing his face ripped open a wound I thought was healed long ago.

Ella stood next to me and read aloud.

We spent many summers here, but you would never swim. You thought you were too skinny because the other kids worked out and played sports. They called you Edward Scissorhands because of your long hair and fingers. So we sat here as you painted people. You know what I loved most about that time, my boy? You taught me to look at people through a different lens. One time you painted a rather chubby boy. In your painting he was thinner with less frizzy hair and a smile that could light up the sky. I asked you about it and do you remember what you said? If so, you'll know the next place to go.

I rubbed the two-day facial hair along my jaw. Raced through memories in my mind, one after another, with no luck. Couldn't remember what I said back then.

"What do we do if you can't remember?" Ella followed me to the car and sat inside.

I closed her door. Pop told me to always open the door for my girl, no matter how many years we were together.

"I got it," I said, turning the keys. "I told him that he could borrow my lens if he wanted."

"Classic Gavin line. How could you forget it?"

"Maybe it was too easy. Just didn't think of it."

"So where does the clue lead?"

"Chickie's Rock."

"What's that?"

"You'll see."

"So, I know this will probably annoy you if I ask, but you've had your fair share of annoying me too." She smiled. "But what makes your dad so different?"

"Different from me?"

"No. What makes him different from everyone else that you refuse to paint him into something beautiful?"

Matt always thought it was funny that I made it a point to have the last word, a sarcastic last word at that. With Ella I couldn't do that. She prodded in places I didn't know existed and always left me speechless. The thing I loved about her though . . . she never forced me to respond. She let her question float between us. No pressure. She knew I'd answer her after I thought for a while.

We parked and walked toward the trail. I looked up and took Ella's hand. "Do you think we'd still think the sky is beautiful if it were green and the trees were blue?"

She smiled. "Maybe. Hard to say. We've already been conditioned to think a blue sky and green trees are beautiful, not the other way around."

"Do you see what I'm saying?" We walked up the trail, shaded by rows and rows of trees.

Ella thought for a while. When we reached the top she inched her way to the edge and held onto the wooden fence. Just a little fence between her and an enormous cliff. She looked down to the train tracks alongside the Susquehanna River. The breeze blew her hair from her face as she inhaled and scanned the scene. Birds flew down from the trees, chirping and flying back to their nests. I loved this nook in the world.

"Have we been conditioned to think this is beautiful, too?" I said, pointing at the bridge to the left. "Or is beauty something we either appreciate or discard? Are we the ones who determine beauty or is it determined for us and we choose how to see it based on our own experiences?"

"Okay." She turned and kissed my cheek. "People always told me I was deep, but I'm pretty sure you lost me there."

"I grew up thinking my father looked like an old man I called Pop. Just because someone is walking into my life and telling me that they're my father, I can't accept it. The sky is blue and I'd never be able to get used to it being green."

"Could you at least paint him in a better light?"

"I don't know. I don't paint people beautiful like Pop said. I paint them as I see them. The boy at the pool was thinner in my painting and had a bright smile, because although he was constantly ridiculed he never stopped smiling. I painted his heart into his stature. That's all. I paint what I see."

"So what are you saying?"

"I'm saying I can look at a model and paint a depressed woman sitting on a mountain of clothes. She's not happy. She's not beautiful inside. I can

84

paint an attractive little boy into a kid with warts and fungus growing out of his ears. I paint the inside on the outside. Pop thought I saw the best in everything around me. I don't, Ella. That's all you. I just see what I see."

"Gavin." She tugged my collar and pressed her lips into mine, then pulled away. "I have an assignment for you tonight. I don't want to go to the next place or even open the letter we dig up here until you do this."

"I can't see him right now. Maybe one day. Maybe after the wedding. Not right now."

"The assignment has nothing to do with him. Just you."

After we ate dinner, Ella took me to the basement and blindfolded me by wrapping one of my long-sleeve t-shirts around my face. After tying it three times to make sure I couldn't peek, she pat my head and walked away. Something clicked in front of me. Then a bang.

"Okay, take it off and look," she said.

I reached for her hand. "Make me."

Her legs touched mine as I inhaled her fruity shampoo. Pieces of her hair touched my arm.

"Ouch," I said, ripping the shirt off my eyes and falling backwards off the chair. "What the?"

She held her stomach and laughed. "Couldn't help myself."

"What did you do?"

"Just a little pinch." She bent over in a fit of laughter.

"You are sadistic." I laughed.

She gave me her hand to help me up, but I pulled her down to me instead. "Kiss me oh sadistic lover."

She tried to kiss me while laughing. And failed. After a few exhales, we stood, still out of breath. She pointed to the mirror in front of me and pushed the chair toward me. "Sit."

I did.

She moved an easel with a blank canvas and set it to the left of the mirror. "I want you to paint what you see when you look in this mirror."

"Can I paint you instead?"

"No. Plenty of those already. Paint yourself. I'll give you a few hours to

85

do so while I finish setting up this art center for the kids."

"When do you plan on opening up for lessons?"

"Next week."

"Are you kidding me?"

She pointed to the mirror. "Stop stalling, Gavin."

I looked at my reflection. To the right she had some water, an array of paints, and a few brushes. Not exactly the ones I would've chosen, but I didn't say that.

I picked up a brush, studied my reflection, and squeezed a few colors onto my palette. Ella smiled. I smiled back. Hands shaking, I dipped my brush into a blob of color and painted what I saw. An hour and fourteen minutes later I sat back, crossed my arms, and told Ella to come and see.

She stood beside me, eyed the painting, then turned and faced me. She surveyed me, then the painting, then me again.

"Doesn't look a thing like you," she said.

I leaned toward the mirror. "It's identical. It was a quick painting, it's not going to be perfect."

She ran her fingers along my brow. "This is more narrow in real life. And this"—she squeezed my nose—"is not nearly as big as you painted it to be. You also painted bumps on your nose. Don't see those here." Her eyes turned back to the art. "Your lips are too thin, ears are too big, and your cheeks look like you are sucking them in."

"Well, now that you've made me feel great about my art skills, what's for dinner?"

"My point is—"

"I know your point."

"Then what is it?"

"That beauty is in the eye of the beholder and sometimes the beholder is blind."

"And?"

"That I need to see beauty in everyone, not just people I feel sorry for or people that I love."

"And?"

"That I need to see myself as more attractive?"

She laughed. "No. What else? Seriously."

"I don't know. You want me to talk to my father and try to find something worth painting in him?"

She nodded. "I am excited to find out what your grandfather has in store for you, but not until you meet your father. You can't move on until you let go of the past."

"Fair enough."

"Really?"

"Yes."

She ran up the basement steps. "Be right back."

I stared at my reflection and the painting. Honestly couldn't see a difference. But I trusted her. It only made sense that I'd see myself in a more negative light than I actually am. Don't we all? We pick apart our flaws and try to improve them more than we sit back and appreciate what we do have. Ella never failed. She always taught me something about life. I hoped I could be the same for her and not some leech who only takes. Like I did to Pop.

She scurried back down the stairs and sat on my lap. "The next letter. Ready to open it?"

"Go ahead and read it."

She unfolded the paper and read.

Flies can be sitting in a garden and completely ignore the beautiful flowers around them. Instead they'll go right for the rotting banana peel or piece of trash. Bees, on the other hand, could be sitting in a room full of trash and find the tiniest speck of fruit or honey to land on. Don't be a fly. Become a bee and stay a bee. Look for the good in every circumstance, even the most horrible and disgusting places. There's always some honey to land on. This should tell you were to go next.

Chapter Thirteen

At Ella's request, we waited to finish digging up Pop's letters until I met Harold Kessler. Only one problem. I deleted his calls and voicemails and had no way to get in touch with him. We decided to wait for him to call, but he didn't. I guess my frantic escape, burning rubber and all, made him back off. Didn't blame him. In fact, that was my intention.

Ella finally told me to call the detective again. I was hoping she wouldn't think of that and we'd be able to move on. I called and told him to tell Harold I'd meet him, with Ella, at Rittenhouse. A beautiful park in Philly. Dotted with trees in the middle of huge buildings.

Ella and I swung our linked hands as we walked through the entrance. Quaint benches sat along the path, waiting for someone's story to sit down and say hello. I wasn't sure I wanted to sit on a bench. Not with the story about to unfold. I led Ella to the grass. We spread out a blanket and waited for Harold to show up.

Ella tossed a peanut at my face.

"Sadistic?" I shrugged.

She laughed. "You were supposed to catch it."

"Perhaps a tiny bit of a warning next time?"

"Watch this." She held out her hand and made a clucking sound. A squirrel clawed its way down a tree to the right of us and inched toward her. Steady as can be, she extended her hand a little further. The squirrel grabbed the peanut out of her hand and ran back up the tree. He perched himself on top of a branch and brought the nut to his mouth.

"Wow." I tried the same. No animals came rushing to me. "Guess you have the magic touch."

"You have to be calm." She squeezed my hand. "Your hands are shaking. They can sense that, I bet."

"Embarrassing."

"Don't be."

We ate a few snacks in silence. Ella watched people and listened to their conversations. So did I. Then I saw him. Turning around in circles in front of a bench. Ella peeked around the tree, then back to me. I nodded and stood. Waved him over to us.

Drops of sweat ran down my face. I wiped them off with my sleeve. Harold put his hands in his pockets and walked toward us. Without a doubt the most awkward moment of my life. Couldn't he walk any faster? My heart ticked in my ears like a bomb. Ella leaned into my arm, looked up at me as I stared at the man in front of me, the man who left me and probably hated me for killing my mother.

"Thank you f-for doing this." He lifted his hands from his pockets.

I wiped my hands on my jeans and avoided shaking his hand.

"Let's sit," Ella said.

I sat down and pulled my knees to my chest. Ella curled up beside me, her legs making a "V" to the right of us. Her squirrel friend zoomed from one tree to another as Harold sat across from us.

"I, um." Harold's eyes darted around, everywhere but me. "I don't know how to say this."

I inhaled, exhaled, tried to remain calm and patient.

"I, well . . . when I . . . I mean, there was a—"

"What the hell did you come here to say?" My knuckles were white and my jaw hurt. From toe to finger I was one huge ball of stress.

"I'm s-s-sorry." He looked down. "I have a b-bit of a, uh, s-s-stutter and when I'm nervous it, uh, it g-gets worse."

Pop.

Ella looked at me. "Didn't your grandfather have a stutter too?"

"Yes." Harold and I answered at the same time.

"I did too," I said, looking at Ella. "That's why I didn't have too many friends and ended up reading books and painting more than socializing. One day I started playing music and singing. Since then my stutter hasn't come back."

Harold nodded. "I got myself into some t-t-trouble and the drugs, they uh, they got me a little worse now. I have a t-t-trouble expressing myself."

Be a bee, I heard Pop say.

"Look," I said. "I'm sorry to be rude. This isn't easy for me and I'm finding it hard to understand why you are here. Why, after all of these years, are you sitting in front of me? Why didn't you just leave me alone?"

"You see, I . . . it's just that when s-s-she died my heart died with her." His head shook as he danced around my question. He readjusted his baseball hat. "I j-j-just came to tell you that I'm s-s-sorry."

Ella saw the frustration written on my face. She reached over and put her hand on Harold's wrist. "Tell me what she was like."

He sighed, choked back tears with a cough. "I'm s-s-sorry. I haven't talked about her since." He touched Ella's hand. "This is the ring I put on her finger, isn't it?"

"Okay," I said. "Can someone please tell me why on earth we are sitting here right now?"

Harold stood. "Didn't mean to waste your time. I just w-w-wanted to tell you I was sorry and tomorrow is, um, it's our wedding a-a-nniversary. I guess I wanted to see the o-o-only piece of her still alive." He swung his arms and tipped his hat. "Nice meeting you miss."

Shoulders reaching for the ground, he walked away. Ella and I stood. She stuffed the blanket back into our bag and tossed the trash into a nearby trash can. I watched Harold until his white t-shirt became a speck in the world. Just another drip of paint on the canvas.

Ella wrapped her arms around me and whispered in my ear. "I love you."

I kissed the top of her head. "I know you feel sorry for him. I hate to admit it, but I do too."

She nodded.

"I will get in touch with him after we finish the letters from Pop. I just need some time. And besides, we have a wedding to plan. I want to focus on us."

LATE SATURDAY AFTERNOON, LYDIA AND SARAH CAME OVER to do girly things for the wedding. Sarah brought her boyfriend and his daughter. Ella convinced me to figure out what happened with his previous marriage. So I convinced Matt to come and play detective. I'm not into prying into people's lives. Makes me feel about as uncomfortable as a fairy at a wrestling match. Doesn't mix.

Everyone arrived about the same time. The girls and Abby made themselves at home right away. While they sat on the living room floor tying handfuls of rose petals in tulle, the guys followed me to kitchen. We grabbed some drinks and sat outside on the patio.

"Needs some work out here," I said, sitting down between the two of them. "Ella wants to make a garden, but since it's a small city yard she wants to keep it pretty simple so we have room for the kids to play."

Matt sucked on an ice cube. "Man, you guys are already thinking kids? Lydia and I aren't quite ready for all that."

"Well, we're not going to have kids right away, but we probably won't wait long. We're both more than ready."

Matt looked at James. "What about you James? Proposing to Sarah anytime soon?"

James leaned back in his chair and pulled the bottom of his t-shirt. I couldn't help but notice the muscles in his forearm. He reminded me of Joaquin Phoenix. He wasn't overly muscular, but definitely made Matt and I look puny. Not what I expected for Sarah. Artists normally go for artist types, not sporty types.

"Did I say too much?" Matt said. "I'm notorious for being a foot in the mouth kind of guy."

"Nah," James said. "I usually don't talk about that kind of stuff. No offense, but I don't know you guys that well yet."

"Yet," I said. "If you plan to marry Sarah you'll be seeing a lot more of us."

Matt raised his water. "Cheers to that."

James didn't look so thrilled.

"So, what do you do for a living?" I asked.

"I'm a gynecologist."

I tried not to spit my drink all over myself. No wonder Sarah kept this guy a secret. Ella would have a fit.

"Oh, really?" Matt said, shifting in his seat. "You don't find it weird looking at other women like that all day?"

"Not at all. A job is a job."

Right, I thought.

"Is that why your other wife left you?" Matt said.

I slapped Matt's knee with the back of my hand. "Well, if you hadn't already put your foot in your mouth there goes your leg."

"I'm kidding." James laughed. "I'm a mechanic. Nothing exciting. Sarah told me about Ella and her ideals. I had to mess with you a little."

I laughed. "My poor Ella. She looks at the world with such love. Everything around her turns into a love story. Even the trees play a part. She may be a tad idealistic in some areas, but honestly, I'd rather err on the side of idealism than settle for less than what that girl has brought to my life."

"Wow, Gavin," Matt said. "Haven't heard you open up like that in, well, I can't even remember the last time."

"Yeah. That's only the tip of an enormous iceberg that would sink not only the Titantic, but an entire continent."

"Could a continent sink?" James said.

Matt laughed. "Anyway, James, what happened with your last marriage? How has Abby handled everything?"

"Did Ella set you up to this?"

"Just wondering. You don't have to answer."

"I've never been married."

"Oh," I said. "Well, what about Abby? Does she see her mother ever?"

"She can't remember her mother or her father."

Matt and I looked at each other.

"Are you messing with us again?" Matt said. "Because that doesn't make any sense to me. I know I'm short on brain cells, but the girl has to have a mother and aren't you the father? She doesn't call you 'daddy' for nothing."

"I am her father," he said. "But she never met her birth parents. My brother and sister-in-law went out on their first date since Abby's birth. My mom watched Abby. She was only about six months old at the time. They were on a canoe. Hit some debris under a bridge. Flipped over. Their bodies were found a week later. Anyway, they died and my parents said they were too old to take the baby. They asked me next since I was the only person left in his family."

"Wow," I said. "Just goes to show . . . you should never judge a book by its cover."

"Sadly too many of us still do, even though that phrase is so popular," Matt said. "So how old were you when you took the baby?"

"I got custody of Abby two days after my nineteenth birthday, three days earlier I got an acceptance letter and scholarship to play running back for the University of Alabama. It was my dream."

"Wow, man." I shook my head. "That's a big sacrifice."

"There's more to the story. I'm not the hero I seem to be." He stood. "But I'm not ready to get into that yet. Maybe another day." He opened the back door. "Sarah has been afraid to introduce me to Ella because she knew it wouldn't be ideal for Ella, but it's hard enough for me to find a woman who will accept this about me. I come with a package deal. So many girls have turned away even after knowing why I have Abby. Sometimes I'd go out and pretend like I didn't have a kid, just to have fun with no strings at-tached."

He walked into the kitchen. We followed.

"So." I closed the door. "Sarah's only hesitancy is Abby?"

He lowered his voice. "She's afraid the cancer will come back and Abby will lose a mother a second time. She can't stand the thought of that so she keeps her heart from me. I know she loves me though."

"I'm so sorry." Matt looked down.

"It will work out," I said.

"Leave it to Gavin," Matt said. "He sees the world through rose-col-ored glasses."

I grabbed another drink. "If only that were true."

"Oh, come on. You are the joyful light bulb that never burns out."

I nodded. Matt looked at me. He didn't quite know what to think when my mind fell to a more reflective state. He knew something was up. Some-thing I never spoke about. I don't know why. Felt like my real feelings were locked in a prison with no bail. There were times I wanted to set them free, but couldn't figure out how. So I'd sit there. Staring through the bars. Waiting for someone to turn the key.

I thought of Tylissa and Mwenye. I know the guy had a sweet personality, but what didn't I know? Sometimes I wondered if he really did have a tweak out moment and kill all those kids. Why else would he admit to it?

"Hey." Ella touched my arm as I leaned into the refrigerator. "Matt and James just came in and said you didn't look so good."

"I'm fine. Just thinking."

"I know better."

"You deserve better, too."

"That's not true at all." She tugged on my hair. "I deserve nothing. You are a gift to me."

"I'm okay. Really. Just want to focus on the wedding and you."

She smiled as a single drop ran from her eye to her nose. I wiped it away and held her chin. We didn't need to speak for me to know what she wanted to say. She loved me. And she wanted me to let go. She wanted me to move on from the past and start a new life with her.

"What I'm about to do is not easy," I said. "And it's all for you."

I kissed her cheek and led her by the hand. Lydia and Sarah looked up from the floor. Still packing petals. The guys eyed me from the couch. I cleared my throat. Counted to three inside. Sliced open my chest. And laid my heart out for everyone to see.

"Most people in this room think I'm a ball of joy just waiting to roll into someone's life. Fact is, I'm not. I'm nowhere close to it. My mom died in childbirth and my dad left me on the side of the road. He disappeared for three decades. And now he's back. Maybe that seems like a good thing, but it's not easy for me and I want nothing to do with him." I squeezed Ella's hand. "But this lady here wants me to try, so I am. All this to say, I'm not who you think I am, but I want to try to be better. I pretend to see the world through positive eyes, thinking maybe if I pretend I will convince myself that it's true. But deep down I'm a mess."

Sarah looked down. Arms crossed. Sadness painted on her face. James watched her as I did. Everyone in the room stood to hug me, except Sarah. After everyone had their turn and talked with me for a few minutes she finally stood. Ella walked over to her. They whispered on the couch for the next hour until everyone decided it was time to go.

She said goodbye to James and Abby and turned to Ella and me.

"Thank you for that, Gavin. I can relate and I think I really needed to hear that." A tear tripped over her eyelid. "I am a joyful person. I know sometimes it is real. I know it is. But sometimes it's not and when you spend your life pretending to be perfect and happy it gets lonely. You realize no one knows you and loves you for who you really are, just the person you're pretending to be."

"Well," Ella said. "I think James does love you for who you really are and I'm happy you found him."

Another tear. "So he told you guys who Abby is?"

"What?" Ella looked at me. "Who is she?"

"He didn't want to tell anyone. I thought he told you."

"He told us," I said. "I'll share with Ella when you leave."

We said our goodbyes and I looked at Ella. Deep into her eyes. Down below Emerald City and into her heart. She knew what I was thinking and blushed. It's not often you find someone you love for better or worse and grow together with them, into one person, into someone better because of it. She was my person. My one person. We were growing into each other. Changing. Morphing into one soul. And I loved every second of it.

Chapter Fourteen

Time flew by. Wedding plans galore. Not to mention our new business, which I have to say, became an instant success. We had a ton of kids and not enough time to devote to each one, so we started offering group lessons for a cheaper price and private lessons for the existing price. After our wedding we planned to find a studio right outside the city. And that would be in a few months. Can't believe how fast time flies.

The weekend snuck up on us and Ella finally decided to revive the letter from Pop and ask me to take her to the next place. So we got in the car and drove off. Lynyrd Skynyrd in our ears, summer sun casting light on our faces, we held hands as I pulled up to Pop's rundown beekeeping area. Untouched for years.

Ella looked around. "Is this his land too?"

"It was. Yeah. He had two-hundred acres."

"Wow."

"I have no idea where he'd plant it here. We took care of the bees together for a few years. Made honey and beeswax candles. We weren't good at it and the bees freaked me out, so we stopped."

She smiled and ran her hand across the old wood. I loved watching her walk. She floated wherever she went. Gentle, long strides. Made me want to take her home and make her my wife right away.

"So," I said. "I know we're pretending to be Willerbean and Mary Lou Dashwood."

She laughed. "Willoughby and Mary Anne. And Willoughby ends up not so nice in the end. He chooses money over love."

"Right. So we are pretending to be a modern day Jane Austen story, but really now, can we pretend to be normal tonight?"

"Normal is relative."

"Normal is a relative to me, not so sure you guys are related though."

She shoved my shoulder and laughed. "You think I'm weird, huh?"

I shrugged and nodded.

"Well, buddy, it's my weirdness that will keep our candle burning when most snuff out and find another light."

"I'm not gonna argue with that, but why can't we just cuddle in bed on a rainy Sunday afternoon?"

"One day you'll look back. Maybe when you're ninety. But it will happen and you will thank me. Trust me." She looked across the hills. "So where's the next letter?"

"Probably by the plum tree." I pointed and we started walking. "But why will I thank you then?"

"Your grandfather liked to plant. Didn't you learn anything from him?"

"What's planting got to do with it?"

"No matter how excited you are when you come home with pots and pots of beautiful plants, you can't just stick them in the ground and expect them to grow. You need to prepare the soil first." She locked her fingers with mine. "So we're preparing our soil. You aren't just anyone to me. You are the one. The only. If we start our lifelong relationship with passion and sex then what would happen when that's gone? When kids come and bills happen? If we don't start as best friends it will be a lot harder to become best friends when hard times come. We will start blaming each other for all of our problems instead of working through them together."

I nodded. Speechless. What could I say to that? Most people I knew wanted passionate and emotional whirlwinds. They couldn't get through a romance novel unless someone had their shirt off by chapter three. Then there's my Ella. Romance was different in her world. In our world. She believed it lived all around us. In the trees, the blue sky hiding behind rain clouds, snow flakes clinging to windshields, squirrels hiding their food, blades of grass catching drops from a misty morning, and in every person to walk the earth. Ella loved to sit on city benches and make up stories about passing strangers. Since meeting her my entire world changed. I always turned life into strands of color on an empty canvas. People blurred by like flashes of light. Just blurs. Then Ella walked into my life and everything slowed down. The blurs of color became people with stories. People with hearts. People. Like me.

She ran her fingers along the arms of the plum tree and stopped at the tip of a leafless branch. "Do you ever wonder what would happen if we broke off all of our dead branches?"

I smiled and nodded. The way I always did when she said something I didn't understand.

She smiled back and squinted her eyes. "What kind of beautiful tree would I be if I cut off all the rotting parts?"

"You already are beautiful."

"Maybe to you, but most of us are more rotten than we realize. Seriously, Gavin. What if I just become a big dead tree that catches fire and turns to ashes?"

"You won't." I knelt down and held out my hand.

She put the shovel on my palm and hung her thumbs from the loops of her jeans.

"What's on your mind?" I said, pulling a ziplock bag out of the ground.

"I'm just wondering."

"Wondering what?"

"Wondering what my dead branches are. It's hard to remove something if you don't know it's there and I don't know . . . I kind of have this fear."

"Fear?"

"What if we find dead branches and you fall out of love with me? What if I can't change and you change without me? What if you don't like what you find inside? What if—"

I stood and pressed my finger over her lips. She closed her eyes. I kissed them and made my way down her cheek to her lips. "And everyone thinks I think too much."

She smiled. "I'm serious. I really fear that."

I cupped my hands around her face and pulled her toward me. "There is nothing that can make me stop loving you. Do you hear me? Nothing."

"But—"

"Nothing."

"I don't want to lose what we have."

"We won't lose this, but it takes work like everything else does. I'm going to fight for you every day of my life, Ella. So relax and let me love you."

She leaned into my chest and wrapped her arms around my back. Her head in one hand and Pop's letter in the other, I stood there and cradled her until the evening sun painted the clouds purple.

Finally, she took the bag and opened the letter. I closed my eyes as she read.

Hey there boy,

Remember when a bee found its way into your suit and you ran around in circles like you'd been caught on fire? Do you remember our talk after that? I told you to stop putting up walls to protect yourself. It's easy to build brick walls, but one day you will want to escape the walls you've locked yourself in and you won't know how. You'll be trying to crawl through holes and find some escape, only to get stuck.

I imagine your walls may be pretty high right now. You've probably let your girl in by now, but what if she dies too? No one on this earth can be everything to you, Gavin. So stop looking for it in others and find it in yourself. There's a beautiful world inside you and it's waiting to be discovered. Sometimes when you build walls you don't realize that other people can see through them. It's yourself you've harmed because you can't see out. So let go please. Let go of your fear of losing people, your fear of being lost. You are not an orphan. You are not an unwanted little boy. You are an adult now and you have to stop letting the little boy inside dictate how you live now.

Let go, Gavin. Do it for me. Don't live the rest of your life wishing the past were different and trying to control your future. You will regret it even more than you regret not coming to see me before I died.

Love,
Pop

PS - your father came to see me before I died. I know you are having trouble with this and I asked him to wait. But now is the time. He has the next letter. It's locked in a box. You will have to bust it open, but I wanted you to know that there's no way for him to read it. Forgive him, and then go get it. Since you probably deleted his address or phone number, here they are.

Chapter Fifteen

Ella and I drove back to our house in Philly without talking much. Exhausted, I walked in and fell back into the couch. She sat beside me and pulled her cell phone from her purse.

"That's weird," she said.

"What?"

"About five missed calls from an unknown number."

"Pennsylvania?"

She nodded. "No voicemail. Should I call back?"

"Maybe? I never call back if I don't know the number, but they called five times."

She pressed the phone to her ear. "This is Ella Rhodes. Did someone call me from this number?" She squinted as all peace vanished from her face. Then she raised her eyebrows and dropped the phone.

I picked it up. "Hello. This is Ella's fiancé. Who is this?"

"I'm sorry, sir. Sarah had Ella as her emergency contact so we are only allowed to notify her. We have disclosed the information to her. She can contact the hospital if she needs more information."

I hung up and pulled Ella's shoulders back to my chest and swept the hair from her face. "What happened?"

"Campfire accident."

"Bad?"

"James is in burn unit and Sarah...." Her voice trailed off into sobs. I held her for a few minutes. Expecting the worst. She wiped her face and looked at mine. "She's severely burned and in a coma."

"Severely burned? From a campfire?"

"They didn't say much. Just warned me that she will look bad if I visit and that her entire body was affected."

"Wow. Should we go visit them?"

"They were taken to West Penn. It's kinda far."

I looked at my phone. "If we leave now we will get there by midnight."

"We can't visit at midnight anyway. We can go in the morning."

"Does that mean you will stay the night?"

She gave me the eyes.

"Let's be honest. I've wanted to make love to you since the first kiss, but I'm not asking for that. I'm just asking for a little lady to get tangled up in my sheets while I dream about her from my couch."

She ran her fingers up my sleeve and squeezed my shoulder. My self-control had its limits and she was walking me along the edge. I closed my eyes as she moved toward me. Her self-control wasn't holding up so well either. I could tell by the way her lips trembled as they lingered on mine. She put her finger on my mouth and kissed around it. I held her head as she squeezed the back of my neck, then stood, taking the road less traveled. At least since about 1920.

"I need to go home anyway for clothes and I want to grab a few things of Sarah's. I will meet you here in the morning. How's eight?"

I stood. "Eight is good."

I kissed her goodbye and stood at the front door until the taillights disappeared. Tomorrow I'd tell her the truth. Maybe in the car ride. Maybe, I thought, I'd make it like a Jane Austen movie. And since I had no idea how, I decided to watch *Sense and Sensibility*, but as I watched I thought of Sarah, pictured her body in flames and my own mortality. I couldn't focus on the movie. At all. Eventually I closed my wet eyes and drifted off to a restless attempt of sleep.

I HEARD ELLA IN THE KITCHEN AS I STEPPED OUT OF THE shower and got dressed. One of the many things I loved about her. The girl could cook way better than anyone I ever met. And she did it with dance and song and a perpetual smile that sweetened my mornings. I loved it so much that I ate most of her creations with her on my lap, feeding me from our shared fork and plate, with a dumb grin on my face.

I walked into the kitchen. Caught her eyes. Her smile. And stored them in my gallery of memories worth coming back to.

She covered a plate with two omelets stuffed with chives, red peppers, kale, homemade home fries, and cheese. Nothing compared to her omelets. Though she'd smile and say it's because of the local organic ingredients. Underneath she knew better. Everything she did, she did well, yet she never gave the slightest hint that she thought well of herself. She never thought low of herself either. Come to think of it, she rarely thought of herself at all.

She scooted her chair so that it touched mine, then wrapped her legs around mine and handed me a fork.

"Your turn to feed me," she said with less joy than most mornings.

She was trying to be normal, but as soon as we saw Sarah she'd lose it.

"There's something I need to tell you," I said. "I was going to try to make it romantic and Jane Austen-ish, but I couldn't get into romance mode with James and Sarah on my mind. So, here I am." I lifted her legs off of mine and knelt on the ground beside her. "I am begging you with all I've got, marry me tomorrow."

She laughed. "Are you talking with your hormones or your heart?"

"I have hormones, don't get me wrong, but I don't let them speak for this." I tapped my chest. "I may not be a smart man, but I know what love is."

"Thank you, Forrest Gump."

"Seriously, Ella. Marry me. Marry me now."

"And give up my dreams of the perfect wedding?"

"Give them up."

She squeezed my hands and smiled. "Okay."

"Yes? Really, Ella? I'm dead serious here."

"We can get married sooner. Something more simple. But I have one condition."

"Anything."

"My maid-of-honor needs to be there."

I sat on the chair beside her. "I agree with you, but that could be months after our current wedding date. If she's as bad as they say, she won't be home anytime soon."

"Really?"

I nodded. We finished eating in silence. Gourmet breakfast on paper plates. Always made me laugh inside. She cleaned up the table. I took out the trash. And we got in the car and headed toward Pittsburgh.

We barely spoke, but kissed at every red light until the cars behind us beeped. A habit we never wanted to break, regardless of how much it annoyed those behind us.

Eventually we arrived. Ella broke the silence in the waiting room. "Should I call Sarah's parents?"

"Wouldn't someone have already notified them?"

"Not sure." She scanned the other faces in the waiting room. "Wonder how Tylissa is doing."

"Yesterday's news for the world is today's nightmare for her."

"Last I talked to her she said Mwenye was still claiming guilt. She's a mess, but she still won't tell me why he is willing to die or spend his life in prison for something he didn't do."

"Well, maybe he really did it."

"I don't know. I don't think so."

"I saw on the news that his fingerprints were all over the weapons."

"Yeah." She looked down. "I just can't imagine."

"Poor Tylissa."

"She is having a tough time. I think she is going to need to go back to work to pay the bills, but she has no family to watch the baby."

"You could do it."

Her eyes glistened as she smiled. "I could?"

"Yeah. We could plan lessons around her schedule or something."

"I'll call her tomorrow. That would help her out so much."

A few minutes later we were told that I couldn't see Sarah since I wasn't family. They weren't going to allow Ella either, but she convinced them since Sarah had Ella down as an emergency contact. I kissed her and watched her as a nurse led her out of my sight.

I looked through photography and art on my phone as I waited. An hour ticked by and I fell asleep. Two hours and seventeen minutes later Ella touched my arm. I opened my eyes only to see hers filled with tears. Hands shaking, she wiped her face and pulled my hand. I stood and followed her outside where we stood under a tree in the pouring rain. The leaves weren't the best umbrella in the world, but we didn't care. She broke down in my arms. I knew she would. Life can surprise us at an moment with circumstances beyond our control. Leaving us breathless and trapped in an ocean of salty tears with no shore to dance on.

Ella and I wrapped ourselves around each other as we drowned in our ocean of life, both of us too tired and sad to look for a plank to support ourselves. But that's okay. For once I had someone to drown with. Tomorrow we'd come up for air and be new people because of it.

As the rain mixed with our tears I heard Pop's words echo in the hidden corners of my heart. "Sometimes we benefit more from letting go than we do from frantically looking for an escape."

Chapter Sixteen

ometimes life felt like one of those books from middle school. You know the ones where you choose the path and ultimately the end of your story. I used to feel like a pawn in the game of life, but not anymore. Life is bigger than that. I'm more than a pawn. I may not be able to control my circumstances, but I can control my reactions to them. And because of that, in a sense, I determine the end of my story.

So, I decided to stop choosing the wrong paths just because they were easier or safer. I decided to stop standing at forks in the road and choosing to sit on benches, going nowhere fast.

I decided to forgive my father.

Ella and I invited him over for dinner. She cooked a fantastic four course meal. Spring rolls first. Then quinoa salad with cranberries and honey lime dressing. A pasta dish that made me like pasta for the first time in my life. And the grand finale filled the house before Harold arrived, tempting me to skip the other three courses and go straight for the peach and blackberry pie. One-hundred percent from scratch. I wish I could say I helped.

She set the dining room up as though we had been married and entertaining guests for years. I helped, which mostly resulted in laughter. I'm an artist. I'm better with designing the napkins than I am setting the table.

We welcomed Harold to dine with us under the chandelier I fixed the day before. Small talk ensued and managed to keep us all chipper and awake for an hour. When Ella brought out the pie Harold held back tears. I noticed. And I noticed Ella notice. And we both knew Harold saw us notice.

"I'm s-s-sorry," he said. "It's just t-t-that your mother made the s-same exact pie every year f-f-for my birthday. It's m-m-my favorite."

Ella placed the pie in the middle of the table and handed us all a warm slice. We wasted no time digging our forks into the gooey goodness.

Ella put her elbows on the table and leaned in. "Tell me about her."

Harold cleared his throat, took a drink of water, and said, "She was, um, q-quiet. Everyone thought s-s-she didn't speak or had n-n-no personality, but with me she would talk m-m-my ears off every night until I c-c-couldn't hold my eyes open. She was g-gentle. Loved me m-m-more than I've ever seen a bride love her groom. I, um, I never f-f-forced my views on her about anything. I l-l-loved her so much I wanted whatever made her h-happy. But she felt the s-s-same about me. Making decisions was easy because I knew she would s-s-support me either way. Not like a lot of newlyweds who argue all the time, trying to get the other to c-c-conform to their way of life instead of just loving them. We had s-s-something good. Real good."

"And that's why you hated me," I said. "Because you found the best gift in the world and I took it away."

Ella's hand warmed mine. Harold looked down, rubbed his face, and shifted in his seat.

"No need to feel uncomfortable," I said. "I forgive you, but I guess you need to decide if you forgive me."

"You were only a b-b-baby, Gavin." He looked into my eyes, then back down. "She made the d-decision. I guess what k-killed me every time I looked at you was that she chose you over m-m-me. Your life was more important to her than living the r-r-rest of her life with me."

"And my life wasn't more important to you? Do you wish you had just aborted me?"

He cleared his throat again. "For a l-long time I did. I've s-s-spent the last twenty years homeless, wallowing in the p-past. The only lovers I've had since your mom have been p-p-prostitutes." He tipped his hat to Ella. "Forgive me, Ella. I've b-b-been on more drugs than I can even name. Who knows what I d-d-did while on them."

"But you seem too intelligent for all that," Ella said.

"Intelligence is n-nothing," he said. "My dad always t-t-taught me that a man can have all the brains he wants, but it's how much wisdom he has that d-d-determines his future."

Ella thought for a moment, then said, "What's that mean exactly?"

I pulled her hand to my chest and said, "When I was a kid I asked the same thing. Pop told me the difference between intelligence and wisdom is that intelligence gets stuck in your brain, but wisdom takes a journey to your heart."

"So it's when you think with your heart?"

"No," Harold said. "That would b-be your emotions. Wisdom is when your heart marries your m-m-mind. It's something unexplainable really. Kind of like love."

"Interesting," she said. "I always assumed wisdom and intelligence were similar. Maybe wisdom just a little more perceptive."

"I wish you could've met Pop," I said. "He would've loved you."

"I agree," Harold said. "Anyway, I have this b-box from him. He t-t-told me to give this to you, but it didn't seem right last time we met." He pulled the box from a plastic grocery bag and slid it across the table. "I better get going."

"Do you have a home now?" Ella said as we walked him to the door.

"I do. My dad gave me some money to get b-b-back on my feet. So, I guess you could say I'm back on my feet."

I watched Harold walk to his car and drive off. Another face in a busy city. Ella leaned into me. I twirled a strand of her hair as we stood in the glares of the sleepy sun.

"You've rubbed off on me," I said.

"Why do you say that?"

"I feel bad for the guy."

"It's sad. He has no one but us."

I nodded and sat on the front steps. Ella sat on the step below and leaned into me. We watched the sun dip behind the horizon. No words needed. Just us.

The streetlights flickered as Ella looked up at me and broke the silence. "I'd like to marry you sooner, but I want to wait until we finish these letters from Pop."

"What about Sarah?"

"The doctors told me she has a small chance of living. Very small.

Possible, but small. If she does live she won't be able to see our wedding anyway. She'll be there for a long time."

I wiped the tears from her face and kissed her forehead.

"I just wish I could take her place. She's been through enough already and the girl has barely complained once in her life."

"I know what you mean, but we can't change what's happened. Any word on James?"

"They said he is adjusting well. I talked with his mom today. She has the little one for now. She said James proposed right before the accident. He texted his family a picture of her hand with the ring on it. Apparently there was a gas leak. They roasted marshmallows and didn't put the fire out, then fell asleep in the tent and the fire caught the gas and went right to the tent."

"Wow. I can't even imagine. Do you think James will still marry her?"

"I hope so, but not many people would want to marry a girl who loses her beauty. I know it sounds bad, but sometimes I wish for her to die so she doesn't have to experience life like that."

"She will be okay. Whatever happens she'll be okay."

I said it, wondering if I even believed the words that came out of my mouth.

We went back inside and opened the box. Weird to go on living when someone close to you is stuck in a coma. Didn't seem fair.

Ella pulled out a few pictures from the box. "Is this you and your grandfather?"

"That's us." I smiled. "He always said we were destined to be together. After my grandma died he could barely go on. He needed something to live for. Then my dad left me and Pop had to take care of me. We were close. Inseparable."

I opened the letter and inhaled so much I nearly broke my own heart. After all he did for me. After all those years. I decided to sit on a bench and ignore him while he took his last breath. All because it was too hard for me to say goodbye.

I handed the letter to Ella and asked her to read aloud.

Down from the Clouds

Dear Gavin,

When I write these letters I sometimes catch myself wanting to write "dear child." To me, an old fool, you'll always be a child. I stop myself though, because you are a man now. Time for you to start acting like it.

You've played a good man on the outside. Great artist, stable jobs, good friends, and a smile that lights up the room. You've been good at hiding behind that smile of yours. Too good if you ask me.

I'm glad you've forgiven your father. That's the one thing I wanted before revealing my will to you. I gave your dad some money before I died, but everything in my will is for you and your future family.

Come to the house when you're ready. The key is in this box if you no longer have yours. The will is in my bedroom, the first box under the tree was empty. Take what I am giving you and use it for good. Don't refuse my one last wish for you. Accept it because you love me.

It's never goodbye, Gavin. Only see you soon. Take care of yourself and live well. No regrets. Death can steal your breath at any time.

I love you always,
Your old man

Chapter Seventeen

Before we knew it another week had passed. Late Friday afternoon Ella and I finished up our last lesson of the day. I never thought I'd use my talents to teach kids, but I actually enjoyed it. Mostly because I got to work with my love beside me, but the kids were a lot of fun, too.

We handed them off to their happy-eyed parents and went upstairs to prepare the house for our friends. Matt wanted to invite his sister, Miranda, over so she could get to know everyone. About a month after Matt's wedding she moved to Philly to be with her boyfriend, but he never included her in what he did and they soon broke up. I'd been looking for an excuse to have some friends over, so I jumped on the opportunity.

We straightened up the dining room and put some snacks and drinks on the table.

"Would you like to come to Pop's house with me tomorrow?" I said.

"Of course." She smiled.

"And then we can get married tomorrow night?"

She laughed. "Actually, I wanted to ask you something. I am completely fine with ditching my dreams of a big regency wedding, but I was thinking about Sarah again. I really want her to be there, if possible. I was wondering if we could wait a few weeks until she comes out of a coma and get married in the chapel at the hospital."

"Wow. That would be . . . interesting."

"It would be." She walked to the couch. "But wouldn't it be worth it?"

I sat beside her. "It would be. I think it's a good idea."

"Oh, and I talked to Tylissa. She said she would love if we could watch Asylia while she works. Probably only Tuesday and Thursday. She found a job through a friend and they are allowing her to work from home the other three days of the week."

"That's good. I was worried she wouldn't get a job with Mwenye's reputation."

"I don't get it. I wish she'd talk to me. She won't tell anyone the truth. Why would he want his reputation and his wife and child's reputation ruined for something he didn't do?"

"I don't know, Ella. Sounds weird. I can't wrap my head around the fact that he is innocent. All the evidence points to him. Why he would kill a bunch of kids in such a gruesome way, I have no idea. It doesn't make sense, but it also doesn't make sense that they have all this evidence and let us not forget that he himself claims he is guilty of the crime. If he really is innocent, then there must be a really good reason why he is willing to sacrifice so much for whoever it is that actually killed those kids."

Someone knocked on the door. We jumped. Then laughed.

I opened the door with Ella by my side.

"Hey, hey," Matt said. "We come with bundles of joy."

"I'm sure you do," I said, ushering them inside to the couches.

"No, really," Lydia said. "We've come with a bundle of joy."

Ella gasped. "No way."

"Yes way," Matt said. "We are having a baby."

"Wow," I said. "What happened to waiting?"

Matt shrugged. Huge grin on his face. Ella and Lydia hugged and immediately started talking about Sarah. Another knock on the door.

"Oh." Lydia came to greet the girls and introduce me. "This is Myra and Evelyn."

"Nice to meet you," Evelyn said, English accent hard to miss.

"Yes. Very nice to meet you," Myra said.

Ella gave them both a hug. "Where are you two from?"

"Evelyn is from the UK and Myra is from the Philippines," Lydia said. "They were my roommates in school. People always called us the Spice Girls because I had reddish hair, Evelyn's blonde as blonde can be, and Myra is Filipino."

The girls smiled and nodded their heads in unison. Both pretty, but not as beautiful as my Ella. No one could compare. Ever. Tons of women had beauty. All of them if you ask an artist like me. But none of them bear the same kind of beauty as the one you call home. It's more than curves and smiles. It's hidden in the eyes. Two women can have a bazillion plastic surgeries and look identical, but no two women can be the same when you look into their eyes. That's where their real beauty is. I could look into Ella's Emerald City and see another life, a world only she knew. That's why I focused so much on the eyes when I painted portraits of others. The eyes are the doorway to the heart.

We offered Evelyn and Myra something to drink and they quickly grew comfortable with Ella. Couldn't help thinking of Sarah and how she should have been here with her fiancé, celebrating life and love with us. I wondered if she could dream while in a coma. Or if she had nightmares of the accident and couldn't wake up from them. Or if she lived in a continual blackness right now while all of us laughed and talked about meaningless things.

Miranda came inside, along with Dee, Ella's old employee from the coffee shop she owned, and two of Dee's friends, Griffin, who apparently didn't have enough skin for all the tattoos he wanted, and Reese, who had a southern accent and reminded me of Justin Timberlake with a tad more facial hair. I thought for sure Miranda would swoon her self silly over him, but as the night progressed she didn't talk much with him at all. The guys stuck with us on the deck and the girls together in the living room.

Finally, the stars salted the ink-covered sky and the ladies came outside with us. Patrick and Heidi gave everyone a hug goodbye. A little late to be out with a baby, I guess. I wondered when Ella and I would be at that place in life.

Lydia sat on Matt's lap. Those two were about as physical as it gets. One leg wrapped around the other, or an arm, or a hand, anything to make sure they were glued together. Ella and I weren't quite like that. We were subtle in public settings. She sat next to me and touched me with her eyes. She had a very romantic, mysterious quality about her. She didn't want the entire world to see what she said is only reserved for me. Kind of like regency era women who only let their hair down for their husbands. Everything regency with Ella. Romance to her was much sweeter and more elegant than the heated Hollywood romances women went crazy over nowadays. I loved that about her. Any woman can pull a mask over themselves and

117

play sexy, but few women are genuinely sweet and delicate. It's a femininity I can't explain. The mind can't grasp things meant for the heart.

Evelyn, who downed one too many hard lemonades, stood in front of everyone and said, "Alright, ladies and gents, I brought a game for us all to play. These cards I'm holding are conversation starter questions, but the trick is you have to roll the dice and count from your left and stop on the person that equals the number you rolled. Then you have to answer the question as though you are that person. They will write down their answer and if you get it right you get a point. If you get it wrong, you lose a turn."

She handed the cards to Lydia. "You start." Then gave everyone a note pad and a pen.

Lydia picked a card and rolled the dice. "Okay. Question is for Griffin. What was your favorite subject in high school?" She gave him some time to write, then said. "I'm going to guess something music-related?"

He smiled. "English. I'm a writer and I always loved writing and books."

Miranda perked up. So did I. Didn't think I'd have anything in common with tattoo central, but apparently stereotypes aren't always right.

Matt pulled a card and rolled. "This should be easy. This is for you Gavin. What is your favorite book of all time?"

"Don't be so sure of yourself," I said and winked at Ella. She knew the answer.

"It's easy." Matt said. "*Oliver Twist* by Charles Dickens."

"Nope," I said.

"Come on. You collect all versions of that one."

"It's my second favorite."

"He's telling the truth," Ella said. My true best friend. "It's *The Giving Tree* by Shel Silverstein."

I nodded. "She's right."

He laughed and handed the dice to Myra.

"My question is for Miranda," Myra said. "Kind of hard. What is your biggest regret?"

I knew the answer to this and so did Matt. Myra wouldn't guess it in a thousand years. I liked the game though. Great way to get to know people. A little intimidating, but still fun.

Miranda wrote down her answer and Myra thought for a few seconds.

"Um, I'm not sure, but I will say hurting someone's feelings?"

Miranda looked at Matt, then me. "It has to do with my little brother. That was a hard one. You should get another try."

"Rules are rules," Evelyn said. "My turn. Okay. Ella, what is your biggest fear?"

"Right now or in general?" Ella said as she linked her hand with mine.

"Right now, I guess." Evelyn waited for Ella to answer and offered her guess. "I'm gonna say your biggest fear is heights?"

Ella smiled. "I wish. Right now my biggest fear is losing my friend Sarah. Not sure if Lydia filled you in, but she was in a campfire accident with her fiancé and burned most of her body. She's still in a coma right now."

Everyone looked down. Except me. And Reese. We glanced at each other and he nodded to Ella and me. A silent way of saying, "I'm sorry."

Ella bit her lip to hold back crying. I pulled her closer and motioned for everyone to keep playing.

Dee picked a card and kept the game going. "Alrighty, Myra, I think I know the answer to this one. Do you believe in soul-mates?"

Myra swept her long black hair behind her ear as a smile softened her face. "This one is too easy. Everyone does."

"Yes," Lydia said. "Myra moved here from the Philippines because she met a guy on MySpace back when that was the cool thing to do. She came here for him, went to college here so she could get an extended visa or whatever that is, and they broke up. When I asked her why she wasn't sad about it she looked me straight in the eyes and said, 'When the right guy comes this guy will seem like a nobody.' And this was before Ella and Gavin's storybook news story."

"Will you go back to the Philippines, then?" Reese said.

"I will have to, but I might come back," she said, blushing.

Reese held eye contact with her until she looked down, face flushed. I looked at Ella. She shrugged and smiled. Too many potential love stories floating around the room tonight. Knowing Ella she'd have them all dating someone before the night ended.

"Okay." Reese picked a card and rolled the dice. "Myra." He smiled and spoke with his charming southern drawl. "What quality do you look for most in a man?"

She smiled and wrote her answer. "Make a guess."

He hesitated, then smiled and said, "American?"

Everyone laughed. She stood and walked over to him, picked up the card with the question, and said, "Katapatan. In English, honesty." She showed everyone the card. "The real question on the card was 'what's your favorite childhood memory?'"

She sat back down, face red as a July sunset, and crossed her legs.

"Well, she got me there," he said. "But at least I'm clever."

We all laughed for a few minutes as the game fizzled out. We ended up talking in small circles. Ella watched the chemistry between Myra and Reese. And I watched her as she watched them. Meanwhile, Miranda grew quiet as the night progressed. Something wasn't right with her, but I figured I'd ask later. We wanted her to enjoy herself and get to know new people. She had a tendency to gravitate toward guys with depression. And she morphed into whoever she was around. Hence the colorful hair and weird clothes. Matt and I called her a chameleon because she changed for every guy she dated and refused to stay single long enough to figure out who she was outside of a man.

A person can want love all they want, but if they don't figure out who they are and learn to love their own self first, they'll never stay in love. They'll marry for the wrong reasons and divorce five years down the road. Inevitable. How can someone love you for who you are if you don't even know who you are? Maybe that was the advice I needed to give myself. Maybe I needed to learn to love myself, all of myself, even the ugly stuff.

After Ella and I escorted everyone out the door I pulled her into me and kissed every part of her face as the half-moon smiled above us. Street-lights in her eyes, cool September night on the brink of a thunderstorm, yes, it took all I had not to scoop the girl up and take her upstairs.

She kissed my lips and tapped my nose. "Getting hard for you, isn't it?"

"I'm guessing it's not hard for you?"

"It's killing me. Not just that. I want to wake up next to you afterward. I want to start our life together."

"So, let's start it then."

"You love me a lot."

I smiled. "Of course I do. What man would endure this weird 1800's relationship style nowadays?"

"Do you really think it's weird?"

"It wasn't weird back then. In fact, back then they barely saw each other at all before they married. So we would be scandalous to those people."

"But you know why I don't want to come upstairs with you right now, right?"

"I do."

"Then why?"

"Because you love me a lot."

"I don't ever want to lose you. You're my best friend. I want it to stay that way forever."

"Me too, love." I kissed her hand. "You mean the world to me. I'll do whatever it takes to prove that to you."

Chapter Eighteen

Since I met Ella we had gone on car trips quite a few times. She is the queen of car trips. She plans snacks, takes care of the GPS, brings various drinks for various moods, umbrellas and boots in case it rains, and even sets up a playlist on her phone to set the mood. It cracks me up every time. She takes it so seriously.

Our trip to Pop's house for the grand finale of his scavenger hunt was no different. Prior to the trip she made me write down the soundtrack of my life. So, I did. Thinking nothing of it. Our trip to Lancaster included those songs. Ella reminded me so much of Pop. They both lived and breathed romance. It went beyond love stories and fused into life stories. They were emotional. Could turn a sunny day into a black cloud or a thunderstorm into a spring morning in three seconds flat. I didn't have that quality, but loved surrounding myself with people who did. They never failed to bring color to every black-and-white canvas.

When we parked in front of the house my heart wanted to jump out of my chest and run off into the woods.

Ella ran her fingers down my arm. "Been a while since you've been here, huh?"

I forced myself to breathe. "Not just that. He died here. In his room. I should've been here, Ella. I wasn't. And the reason I wasn't here—"

"Is because you were with me."

"It was the night I saw you on the news. I got a call from the nurse that he wasn't doing well and would probably die within a few hours. I chose to search Philadelphia for you instead of going to his side. He died with no family around. No one except his nurse. Yes, it was hard for me to deal with losing him and I avoided his sickness for a long time. Made myself believe he'd be okay. I ignored his letters. His calls. I acted like a child. And that night I got the call from his nurse right before I walked into my apartment, I was just in Lancaster for a job interview and considered driving right back to be with him. Then I sat down on the couch with Matt and Lydia and saw your face on my television screen. Honestly, I didn't remember Pop until the next day and it was too late."

"I'm sorry, Gavin." A tear zig-zagged down her cheek. "Let me take the blame. Don't be so hard on yourself."

"It wasn't your fault. It doesn't matter anyway. He would've told me to go after you instead of coming to him. I just feel horrible. If I would've just answered one letter or call."

"It's over now." She kissed my cheek. "There's nothing we can do to change the past. Let's go inside. I want to see where you grew up. And if he is giving us this house, you are going to have a real tough time convincing me not to live in it."

We walked up to the porch. My sweaty, shaky hand in hers. My best friend. The person who would walk through the good, the bad, and the ugly with me for the rest of my life. I loved her. Quite possibly more than I did five minutes ago.

I reached for the key, but Ella noticed it was already cracked open. She pushed it as my heart sank to the ground and a million balloons flew at our faces. Or at least what seemed like a million. We stepped back and watched them float past the trees, into the sky, until they became tiny specks on a sheet of blue.

We smiled and turned back to the door. A large piece of fabric hung from the top. I guess it was there to hold the balloons in place until the door opened and pushed them all toward us. I analyzed the set up, wondering how it worked so well, until Ella pointed on the floor.

A note. Taped onto the shiny hardwood. Pop's handwriting.

So, you've found love, but don't forget love starts within and then crawls from your heart into the lives of others. Love doesn't end with the person you're standing with. It seeps into the lives of your children, your friends, and even strangers. Love is all around us, all the time. Just like the sky that those balloons made their way to. On cloudy days it's easy to forget, but all you have to do is a catch a ride on a plane to see that the blue sky is always there. It just takes a little break sometimes. Without the rain the flowers would never grow. We need a break from the heat sometimes. Love is like that too. Even when it's cloudy, it's still there. It's up to us to choose to live by this love or to love our own opinions and desires too much to ever notice those around us. This wasn't what you did, Gavin. Forgive yourself, move on, and know that I know ... more than anything in the world ... how much you've always loved me.

I grabbed Ella's arm to balance myself and tried, with every ounce of manliness inside of me, to keep the tears behind my eyes. I fell to my knees, kissed the note, and stayed there, trying to forgive myself.

Ella knelt beside me. "Gavin."

I nodded. "I'm okay."

"I know, love. But I want to tell you that it's okay to not be okay sometimes. It's okay to cry."

I stared into her eyes and saw a heart so big it could crush this town. That was all it took. A few days ago she broke down in my arms. Now it was my turn. Tears wetting her shoulder, she held me. She held me until I cried every tear I held inside for the last thirty years.

Memories. They faded in and out of my mind without my permission. Learning to swim with Pop by my side. Going for long walks in the woods and catching cray fish. Planting a bazillion trees. Dancing to Elvis in the living room. Reading aloud at night by the fireplace. Cutting the grass and getting rushed to the hospital when the blade hit a piece of metal and sliced open my calf. Learning to drive and hitting a parked car. Graduating high school. Going to college. Pop was there for it all. Every important memory. He was by my side.

An hour later, I stood and wiped my eyes. "Well, now I have a headache."

She smiled. "I love you."

"I love you, too." I inhaled deeply. "I'm sorry. I feel like a fool."

"Don't." She touched my cheek. "Haven't you heard the saying, 'real men cry?'"

"Yeah, doesn't mean they cry like babies for an hour on the floor. A few tears would have sufficed."

"This is good. I'm so happy for you. This is so good."

"Let's go get this will. I have a feeling we're going to end up living here."

We walked up the wooden stairs, still in perfect shape, still as clean as the day I left. Ella wanted to see my room first, so I showed her. Pop left a lot of things the same. I stayed in that room when I visited and he wanted me to be comfortable. Golden honey walls. Natural wood trim. White window seat and curtains. Cream blankets and sheets. My home for so many years.

She ran her hand along the bookshelf. "Are all of these yours?"

"They are. I only took my favorites. Figured that alone would be more than the average person has on their book shelf."

"Probably right." She sat on the bed. "Any other girls ever sit on this bed with you?"

"Just Matt's sister, Miranda."

"You two seem close. No history there?"

"Not at all. We were close though. Matt and Miranda were pretty much best friends. They had one of those ideal brother and sister relationships. Big brother protected little sister. Little sister adored big brother. She was always, always getting herself into trouble and Matt and I spent many nights talking her out of way too many things."

"Can't believe she never had a crush on you."

"Not everyone thinks I'm as wonderful as you do."

"Hard to imagine." She walked to the window. "What a view."

"Perfect view for inspiration. Faces the south so it's always bright in this room. I spent many days and nights reading and painting and writing while sitting on that window seat."

"It's beautiful."

I took her hand. "Let's go to Pop's room. I'm all cried out, so don't expect me to break down again."

We laughed and walked the creaky hall to Pop's door.

"You gonna open it?" she said.

"Maybe."

"Want me to?"

I held the doorknob, took a breath, and shoved the door into the wall. Definitely didn't mean to do that, but nothing could've shocked me more than what I saw next. Pop flung straight up in his bed. Face pale. Eyes wide as the ocean. Ella screamed and jumped behind me. Pop laughed. My jaw fell to the floor and stayed there.

I grabbed Ella. "Do you see what I see?"

"His spirit is here." She took another step back. "I don't like this."

Pop, or his spirit, bent over in a hysterical fit of laughter.

"Is this some kind of joke?" I said, imagining scenes from *A Christmas Carol.*

The thing that looked like Pop stopped laughing and held out his hands. "Well, I'm real. Touch and see," he, it, whatever it was, said. "This isn't how I expected this to go, but you swung that door open so fast it woke me right out of a dream and scared the daylights out of me."

"A dream? You're dead. What the hell is happening?"

"It's me, Gavin. Come on, now. Did you really think I'd die without saying goodbye? I've known for years this is how you would react to my death, so I knew I'd have to do this to you to get you to wake up and move on with life. Plus, I didn't want you living with regret for the rest of your days. I had to do this. Don't you see?"

Ella's hand finally fell from her mouth as my fists loosened. I closed my eyes, opened them, and closed them again.

"Am I dreaming?" I said.

"Gavin." Pop laughed. "I'm real. Get over here and hug me."

I looked at Ella. She nudged my back. A few steps forward, a few back. I couldn't process everything. The man I thought was dead, the biggest regret of my life, the person I'd been avoiding for months and months . . . alive? Really alive? This would go down in history as either the most amazing thing ever or the cruelest prank in the world.

He waved us over. "Come and sit with me. We have a lot of catching up to do. I saw your story on the news. Ella, come and sit too."

She stepped toward the bed. He hugged her and gave her a pat on the head, then moved toward me. His arms wrapped around me, pulling me toward him, into the bed alongside him. I collapsed in his embrace, feeling like a five-year-old again, laughing so hard I cried. Tears of joy. Unexpected, unbridled joy. Never in a million years could anyone have pulled this off. No one except Pop. Or maybe Ella.

I took a step back. "How did you manage this? They said you had a month to live."

"They told me last year that I would probably have six months. The cancer went crazy inside and they suggested this and that treatment. I stopped chemo and radiation. Stopped going to the doctor. I don't want to die that way. I'm ready to go now. I've lived plenty. I needed to get you straightened out before I left and I stayed here hoping you'd make it before I died." He held is chest. "After that scare just now I think it may be any day now."

"So did you plant all those boxes and notes right before we dug them up?"

"Some of them, but it took you a while to get to the next one sometimes. I'd check every so often and one would still be there. I had some help too."

"We've had a lot going on." I looked at Ella, her face one huge brilliant ray of light. "Started a new business together. Planning our wedding. Ella's best friend was in a camping accident and severely burned."

"It's hard for me to walk," Pop said. "But let's go down to the trees and talk a little."

We helped him out of bed and down the steps.

"How did you bury all those notes as weak as you are?" Ella said.

"Well, like I said, I had a little help. Remember though, you can be dying on the outside, but the only thing that matters is how alive you are on the inside. You'd be amazed at the things a dying body can accomplish when the heart is filled with love."

"I always thought you couldn't wait to die since grandma died," I said as we walked outside and into the grass.

He grabbed my hand. Gripped as hard as his frail hand could. "You were always worth living for. Besides, your grandma would've wanted me to be with you. She never got to meet you. I really think having you helped me live when my heart wanted to give up."

I held Pop's left arm. Ella held his right. Together we walked in peace.

Slow and steady. Down the hill we used to race down when I was a kid. Memories flashed through my mind like an old black-and-white film one still frame at a time.

We reached Pop's trees. His and grandma's favorite. Zelkova trees with enormous trunks and twisting branches. Pop sat in the shade on a wooden bench, white paint chipping off from years of wear. We sat beside him as he caught his breath. It wouldn't be long now, I thought. He was at peace. He finished what he set out to do and I could already see the darkness creeping in.

We talked for hours on the bench. At times I'd get so excited that I'd end up pacing around the tree and talking with my hands. Ella smiled the entire time. Pop did too. Whenever I stood he held her hand as though she were his own grandchild. Matt always said I was the balloon in his life and he was the weight that kept me down. For once in my life I felt like that were true not only on the outside, but the inside too.

Pop knew me so well. He knew I needed this. I needed to live from my heart. From the place he and Ella knew so well. And he knew it wouldn't have happened unless I was broken first. So he broke me. And then, as we sat in the shade on an amber September night, watching the sun fade behind the trees, Pop took my broken pieces and molded them into something new. Something deeper. More beautiful. Colorful. He molded me into a person with desire and life. A person who stopped to smell roses and climb trees. A person who didn't take life for granted.

A person like him.

Chapter Nineteen

The next few weeks were a whirlwind. Ella and I spent a lot of time with Pop as his health quickly declined. He went over his will with us. Gave us the house and told us we could sell it and keep the money, or live there mortgage-free. Acres upon acres and a huge house completely paid off. Ella already imagined our future children running down to the same trees I grew up climbing. I wasn't so sure at first, but she talked me into it. Well, actually, she challenged me to a tickle fight where she made the craziest motions, like some kind of dying hyena. I laughed so hard I could barely stand. Easy win for her.

Pop asked if we could move in before he died so he wouldn't die alone. I think he enjoyed Ella's presence. The soft presence of a woman. She'd just sit there and read books to him. He loved it. I did too. I'm so glad they got to meet each other after all.

So, we gave our art and music students a three week notice of cancellation and advertised for Lancaster. Pop's house had a small guesthouse that would make a perfect studio. Already had fifteen students registered for November and we hadn't packed our stuff yet.

Ella insisted that we get married before moving in together. So we had one month to do so and Sarah was still in a coma.

They moved James to a different part of the hospital. Not completely sure how it all works, but Ella told me they were working with him in a therapy unit. We could visit and talk with him. So we did.

When we got there he smiled. Looked the same as he always did, except his arms and legs had been burned. Face looked great. Just one small mark near his left ear and neck.

Ella's voice shook when she spoke. We made normal small talk for a few minutes, then James put an end to it.

"It's my fault," he said. "I should've put the fire out. I wasn't thinking. When the tent caught fire I jumped up and ran out without thinking. Like a dream or something. I forgot about her." He shook his head. "Then I went into the flames to get her and it was too late. She was covered in flames." His lip trembled. "I rolled around on the ground with her to get the flames off of us. It was my fault. Seeing her like that. I did that to her."

"It's not your fault, man," I said. "You can't beat yourself up about it. It was an accident. These things happen. You can't dwell on it."

"I'm good at dwelling. The last words I said to my brother were in a text right before he died. I'm the reason he went over the line. We were fighting. My last words to him were two letters. 'F U.' I saw his iPhone go from blue iMessages to green text messaging within seconds. I assumed he turned his phone off to ignore me. I will never forget the way my mother broke down when the cops came to the door to tell us he was dead." His tone carried weight as he talked. Lots of weight. Too much for one man to bear. He continued, "I killed Sarah. Even if she wakes up, I killed her spirit. Most of her skin was burned and a few organs were affected. If she wakes up she has a long road to recovery. I don't want her to wake up. I don't want her to suffer because of me."

He yelled at himself as he told us the rest of his story. When he finished, Ella and I looked at each other. She motioned for me to say something. I couldn't have found a word even if someone handed me a dictionary. So I looked down and let the silence kill his anger.

For a second I thought peace returned to him, but he flung his body back and forth and screamed to the top of his lungs. Nurses flew in. Ella explained what happened. They told us to leave the room. As we walked away James shouted over and over, "Let her die. Just let her die. And take me, too."

Sobering, to say the least. Ella and I drove back to Philadelphia in complete silence. No music. No talking.

I thought of my dad. So glad Pop cracked my heart open and poured a little of it into my dad's life. Holding grudges made me feel justified for a little, but that kind of anger and bitterness never dies and the only person it would've killed would've been myself. The people we choose not to forgive will move on. They'll get over it. Meanwhile the person who refuses to forgive is like a tea bag steeping so long that even ten spoons of sugar wouldn't make the bitterness worth drinking. I didn't want to be the drink no one wanted to swallow.

Then there's James. What do you tell someone when the one person they can't forgive is their own self? I guess I could relate.

ELLA AND I FINISHED UP THE LAST OF OUR LESSONS, MOVED all of her stuff into Pop's house, and moved her in with him as well. He liked that idea. Yes, it put her an hour-and-a-half away from me, but it wouldn't be for long.

On an usually pleasant sixty-five degree October afternoon Ella and I had a picnic on Pop's land, our future home, down by the creek. We talked about Pop and Sarah. What to do about the wedding. Then, Ella got a call from a Pittsburgh number. Within minutes, we were in the car.

Three months and six days after Sarah and James got into the accident, she woke up to a new season of life. Ella could visit, but they still wouldn't let me. Not until they moved her to a different part of the hospital. When we arrived I kissed Ella and wiped her eyes, "Be strong, okay? Don't let her see you cry. She needs us to tell her everything will be fine right now. There will be other times to cry with her. That time isn't today."

"I'll try," she said, lip shaking. "This isn't going to be easy."

"I'll wait here as long as you need me to. Don't feel rushed."

She rounded a corner, wiping her tears onto her sleeve. They would take her away and dress her in a gown, gloves, and a mask. Required for all visitors of burn patients to avoid infections. I watched the clock for a while, but when the minutes turned into an hour and the hour turned into two hours, I got up and walked around. Ella happened to walk out a few minutes later, head buried in her elbow. Maybe it's cheesy. Maybe everyone would think it was strange. I didn't care. I picked her up and let her hide her tears in my sweater as I carried her to the car.

We stood next to the curb. I gazed into Emerald City. A little darker there tonight.

"Did she remember you?" I said.

Ella nodded. "She remembered everything and everyone."

"Does she know what happened to her? That she's burned pretty bad?"

She shook her head and tried not to cry. "Gavin. I don't know how. Don't understand it at all. The girl just got over a bout of cancer, possibly lost her chance to have children, finally gets engaged to a man who really, really loves her, and she's lying there on this hospital bed, looking like a mummy. Something out of a horror film really. She can't move. All I can see are her eyes, lips. and toenails. And she knows she's lost her face, her body. She knows she has a long road ahead of her. And what does she do, Gavin? While I'm holding back tears, trying not to lose it, what does she do?"

She stopped to catch her breath. I waited.

"What?" I said. "Everything okay?"

"She whispered, 'Ella, is that you?' Her eyes were closed. I told her it was me and she said, 'Please, don't worry. Remember what I told you before? A spoonful of sugar helps the medicine go down.'" Ella sniffed. "Can you believe that?"

I smiled. "With Sarah, yes, I can believe that."

"I don't think she will be able to see us get married. I asked if we could do it in her room. We can't. So I'm ready whenever you are."

"Okay," I said, opening the car door for her. "Let's not think about that today. We can talk about it later."

Chapter Twenty

The night before our wedding Pop's body weakened even more. He could no longer move or speak, but he could hear and nod a little to communicate. We didn't think he'd make it through the night, so Ella insisted I stay. Our first night together. Besides the few hours at the park. Not the best circumstances, but it actually was romantic. Pop asked us to light candles in his room, especially the lavender beeswax candles. My grandma's favorite. Then he directed us to a box in the closet. Top shelf. Furthest back. I pulled it down and looked inside. Tons of letters. Hundreds or thousands of them.

"Want me to read these?" I said.

He nodded.

I sat beside his bed. "Can Ella and I take turns throughout the night?"

He nodded.

I sifted through the letters. Didn't take long for me to realize what they were. Ella reclined in the chair next to Pop's bed, held his hand, and closed her eyes.

The letters were divided by year. Obviously he saved them in chronological order. I held the first one by the flickering light of a candle and read aloud.

October 30, 1929
My dearest love, my Miriam,

Yesterday most of the world experienced something negative with the stock market, but I barely caught wind of it because my heart was set on you. You probably think I'm crazy. I'm sure you give hundreds of guys your address every day. I'm no different than most of them. Nothing special here.

I haven't been able to get you out of my mind since the moment you walked into the room. Your black dress and coat. Your dark hair pulled up and under a red hat. Single pearl earrings. I've painted you in mind so I always remember the day I fell in love with my wife. Maybe I'm bold, but when you know, you know....

I hereby proclaim this the first letter of hundreds. Care to write the greatest romance in the world with me?

If so, write back.

Eagerly awaiting your response,
Edward Kessler

November 10, 1929
Dearest Edward,

I find it quite silly that you questioned my affections. Did I not give it away with my constant blushing and childish grins?

I found myself thinking of you every day since we first met. Of course I will write this love story with you. Even when we are old and gray with many grandchildren, our feeble hands barely able to hold a pen, I will still write to you. Let's promise to always write letters to each other, regardless of the difficulties we face.

When you know, you know....

Most affectionately yours,
Miriam

Ella drifted to the land of sleep as I continued reading aloud. Every now and then Pop nodded and grinned. As far as I could tell, he never fell asleep, so I kept reading through their Great Depression romance. Their wedding, several miscarriages, and so much more. All before the 1940's started. Their deep commitment to each other even through disagreements, which I read about several times, amazed and inspired me. Ella woke up when I reached the mid-forties. She took over the letters and I took her place beside Pop. Didn't take long for me to fall asleep to her sweet voice.

When I woke to bands of sunlight lying across the room, Ella had a huge smile on her face and tears in her eyes.

"Did you finish them all?" I said.

"Yes. All the way up to the last one. He kept writing to her after she died. Every Sunday they would walk down to the Zelkova trees and sit on the bench. They'd talk for hours, even when your dad was a baby. So every Sunday after she died he sat there on Sunday and wrote her letters."

"I remember him doing that."

Pop rustled, tried to open his eyes a little.

"Morning, Pop," I said. "Do you need something?"

He nodded to the left of him where two letters were partially hidden beneath his pillows. One read *To Ella and Gavin* and the other *My love, My Miriam.*

Dearest Gavin and Ella,

As I write this you two are probably embracing for the first time. Matt called and told me about Ella being on the news and you racing around Philadelphia trying to find her. Yes, Matt knew I wasn't dead. Did you really think I could dig all those holes as old as I am? I needed help. He's been a good partner. He's a good friend, Gavin. Keep him around.

Anyway, I'm writing this in case I can't speak anymore when the end comes. If I can speak, I probably already told you this. If not, here are my last wishes:

1) if I am still breathing, don't care how bad off I am, I want to be at your wedding

2) invite your father and please, be his son when I'm gone. As much as you have always thought of yourself as some kind of dark cloud, you are not that. You bring sunshine to everyone around you. The best part is you don't realize it. Your father could use some sunshine.

3) put this last letter to your grandmother on her grave right after you bury me. It's also for you to read, but not until I'm buried beside her.

Never give up, you two. Hard times are bound to come. No relationship is perfect, but if you soften up and allow yourselves to mold into one person, instead of two separate people sharing a home, you will find it much easier and more beautiful.

Be one and let no one tear you apart.

Gavin, thank you for lighting up my life after Grandma died. You have no idea how much you helped me live and love again. You are so much like her.

Ella, I'm so glad I got to meet you. What joy you have brought to Gavin's life. I still remember the first time he saw you a decade ago. He called me after work that night and talked about you for an hour. Within minutes of seeing you, he lost the receipt with your number on it and the search began. I hope he never stops pursuing you. You are a sweetheart. You will be a great wife.

Love you both always,
Pop
Edward Kessler

Chapter Twenty One

We didn't invite too many people to the wedding, so it didn't take long to prepare. Ella and I did everything together. She wanted to get married by the Zelkova trees, where my grandmother was buried, and instead of chairs she wanted everyone to sit on blankets in the grass. So we put a basket under the trees with a sign that said, "Make yourself at home."

Ella put bags of rose petals in another basket. She made a little tag for each one. Each tag had a copy of a drawing she made me create and the words, "And so . . . Life begins. Gavin and Ella Kessler. October 28th."

She placed a picture of Sarah on the bench under the trees and sat beside it for a minute.

"Things never turn out the way they look in our dreams," she said.

"It's not easy to get married while she's in the hospital," I said. "But my real dream is to wake up to you tomorrow and every day after. I don't care about fancy dresses and wedding receptions. I don't even care who comes. I want to be yours and I want you to be mine. I don't know about you, but my dreams are coming true today."

"I love you." She smiled. "My brother said he will be here. He's driving from Virginia. Couldn't get ahold of my dad. My mom said she can't make it."

"Are you okay with that?"

"I knew it would be the case. Our family hasn't been close since they divorced. Anyway, since your dad is coming I would like him to escort me to you. I know it would mean a lot to him."

"Well, I have to say I feel a little weird about that."

"Do it for me?"

I nodded. "Is it possible to say no to that face?"

"Many people have." She took my hand. "But you just so happen to love me more than those people."

I laughed. "Definitely true."

We walked back to the house to get ready. A brisk October day. The man we hired as the officiant called an hour beforehand to make sure we were on schedule. We were.

Ella asked me to wear the suit I wore the night we met, but I had other plans. It took me a while to get dressed, even longer than Ella, but she stayed in her room, unseen, until I went outside.

Matt walked up the sidewalk to the porch.

"First to arrive," I said. "A good best man."

"Mad at me for not telling you Pop was alive all along?"

"A little, but I needed it."

Lydia tried not to laugh. "What on earth are you wearing?"

I spun around and faced them again. "I'm prepared to be ridiculed. It's a surprise for her. Might be weird to you guys, but she will love it."

"Are you some kind of Mr. Darcy from *Pride and Prejudice* or something?" Lydia said.

"Something like that." I laughed. "She loves all things regency and old-fashioned. Anything at least a hundred years old. She doesn't know it yet, but the wedding band I found for her is an antique ring from 1880."

"You're something else," Matt said. "Who is coming today?"

"Not too many people. You guys, my dad, Heidi and Patrick, Tylissa, Miranda, not sure about your brothers, and then Ella's brother, Derek, will be here." I counted my fingers. "I think that's it. Oh, and Dee."

"Can I go up and see Pop?" Matt said.

"Actually, I need you to help me bring him outside for the wedding. We have a cot set up outside for him. He wants to be there."

By the time we got Pop settled outside everyone else grabbed a blanket and had taken a seat on the ground. I greeted Ella's brother, Derek, and introduced him to everyone. The officiant, Mr. Wellington, also arrived. I showed him where to stand and asked Harold, still couldn't call him dad, to bring Ella down.

As he walked up the grassy hill and out of sight, my palms shook as I asked Matt to come stand with me. I didn't expect myself to get nervous with such an intimate setting, but I had waited for this moment my entire life. Years ago, when I found her and lost the receipt with her name on it, I thought for sure I'd never see her again. But she waited for me. And I couldn't wait to spend the rest of forever with her.

My Ella.

Matt tapped my shoulder. "Could you look any happier?"

"Shhhh . . there she is."

My bride. She stood at the top of the hill with my dad.

My heart quickened. She nodded to Tylissa, who handed her baby to Lydia and stood, picked up a violin from behind a tree, and began to play *Canon in D*. The same song Ella played the night I finally found her.

She walked toward me. I tried to take in the picture and store it for later. Her antique-looking regency dress sparkling in the sun, hair swept up with two white flowers, October trees of various colors in the background. Perfect.

She stopped and stood in front of me, face bright as her dress, a single tear just below her left eye. She mouthed the words, "The best things come to those who wait."

I took her hand, glanced over at Pop, five-feet from us, lying on his back with a smile clinging to his cheeks, then looked into the eyes of the woman who far surpassed my dreams.

I tried to stop myself, believe me, but once I let the first tear out the rest followed without my consent.

"You're beautiful," I said, squeezing her hands.

Mr. Wellington stepped toward us. With tear-drenched smiles, Ella and I said our vows and pledged our faithfulness to each other. Our eyes were locked. The people around us disappeared. I could hear Mr. Wellington as he asked us to repeat our vows. I loved this woman with every part of me and wanted nothing more than to make her the happiest wife in the world.

"Gavin?" Mr. Wellington said. "You hear me?"

"I'm sorry," I said. "What do I say next?"

Everyone laughed.

Ella placed her index finger over my lips. "You say nothing. Just kiss your wife."

My body warmed with anticipation from my head to my toes. I held her hands in mine and turned to face our friends and family.

"Before I kiss my beautiful wife," I said. "I want to say something. A few months ago we had a pretty serious talk in the car. She asked a bunch of hypothetical questions about love and soul-mates and then turned to me, sweet innocence in her eyes, and asked, 'What is love?' We were silent after that. I didn't know what to say. Maybe she didn't either. So we let it go unanswered. Today"—I turned to Ella—"I want to answer that question."

I took a deep breath, looked at Pop behind Ella, still smiling, and continued, "Love is more than a feeling or a thought. It can't be summed up by a dictionary or disregarded when emotions are absent. Love is not abstract. It's not complicated. It's simple. Beautiful. Love is you, Ella. I've seen the way you dance while making pancakes. The way you twirl my hair when I'm driving. The way you admire trees and flowers and ladybugs as though they were an extension of your very person. For the last few months I've watched you. I've taken in every part of you that you allowed. I watched the way you tenderly held Tylissa's baby and rocked her to sleep. I've seen you put your best friend before your own desires when you were set on getting married in a hospital just so she could be there.

"You have shown me, along with that man over there, that life and love aren't as far apart as we think. They go hand-in-hand, like you and me. You can't have one without the other. Everything around us, inside of us, is love. It's in the birds and the rivers, the newborn baby whimpers, and yes, the passionate kisses we share. Life is a package wrapped up in love. To experience love, we have to open it. Carefully. And cherish every gift we're given.

"So, my darling, I don't know if this answer will suffice. Maybe my regency attire inspired it, because this isn't rehearsed. Just know that I love you. I'm so excited to be your husband. Thank you for being the best gift I've ever received. Thank you for being you. And for teaching me what true love is."

I wiped the tears from her face and kissed her salty lips. Seconds later, I kept kissing. And kissing. And kissing. When we finally opened our eyes all of the guests were up at the small reception by the house. Someone even took Pop.

Ella looked up at me, Emerald City brighter than ever, and said, "Guess

the world really does disappear when we kiss."

I kissed her again. And again. And again.

"Later," she said, and led me to our guests. "By the way, I absolutely adore you in the Mr. Darcy outfit."

"And you completely took my breath away with your little regency dress here. Where did you get it?"

"I sewed it."

"And I continue to discover who you are."

We greeted everyone one at a time, talked about this-and-that, and waited until the sun disappeared behind the earth. When it did, we said our goodbyes out front and watched our friends drive off.

"Did you notice something?" Ella said.

"What do you mean?"

"Miranda's car is still here. She left with my brother."

I laughed. "We inspired them."

"Apparently." She smiled and inched toward me. "I love you, Mr. Kessler."

"And I love you, Mrs. Kessler." I picked her up and carried her through the front door. "And so . . . life begins."

We checked on Pop. Completely at rest. Then I carried Ella to our bedroom down the hall. A little strange to have our honeymoon with Pop down the hall, but we didn't want to leave him. She clung to my neck as I set her down on the bed. Then, she pulled me down to her, a bazillion red rose petals surrounding our new marriage. Our new life together.

With such softness and beauty, she loosened her hair. It fell and curled around her shoulders and neck.

Candles lit our bodies as we kissed to the beat of rain hitting the window. I started with her forehead and kissed my way to her toes, undressing her as I went. Our hands locked above her head, and we kissed again, our love expressed in ways she never allowed before. I knew what she meant now. I can't even describe the meaning and beauty as we made love for the first time, not like two bunnies ready for action, but two best friends ready to become lovers.

We made love. For an hour. Then, even better, she snuggled her warm body against me, draped her leg over mine, and pressed her face into my neck. The feeling of melting into one.

Her breathing slowed as I ran my fingers along her arms until she fell asleep. After a few minutes, I moved my head back, kissed her eyelids, and whispered, "Goodnight, my love," then watched her sleep. Hours passed. I couldn't stop looking at her. How did I get here? How did I deserve this? The candles burned themselves out by the third hour. Our bodies, draped in moonlight, inhaled and exhaled to the same rhythm. I know because I made sure of it, matching her sleepy breaths with mine. My eyes could barely stay open, but I couldn't fall asleep, even when I tried. Too excited, too undeserving, I stared at her, silently promising her I'd never let this excitement die. Ever.

As Dr. Suess himself said, "You know you're in love when you can't fall asleep because reality is finally better than your dreams."

Chapter Twenty Two

Two days after the best day of my life, Pennsylvania's wind brought snowflakes and sleet. Ella and I lit the fireplace in Pop's room and stayed up all night with him. He took his last quiet breath at 5:57am on November 1st. It's almost as though he didn't want to face another sunrise without his love.

Ella and I didn't cry as we watched him drift away from this life. We smiled. Thinking of all the memories he wrote on our hearts. We decided to turn his love letters into a book. Not necessarily to publish. Just for our own family as we continued their legacy of love.

We told a few people about the funeral. Just a few and the newspaper obituary, of course. We planned for a hundred or so people to come to the house, so you can imagine our astonishment when thousands of people gathered around his grave as we lowered him into the earth, beside his bride, under the Zelkova trees, where he belonged.

Ella and I decided that we would be buried beside them one day. Hopefully. We saw how easily our own plans for life can be steered into another direction without our approval.

Harold, Ella, and I stood together and greeted each person. The line took three hours to get through and we heard even more amazing stories about Pop. A true selfless man who knew how to live life from the heart.

After everyone left, Ella and I went back to his grave, covered in fresh dirt and topped with tons of letters and flowers. We found his letter to my grandmother hidden beneath everything.

Ella covered her head and neck with her scarf, scooted under my arm, and asked me to read. Shivering, I opened the letter and read.

September 15th
My dearest, precious Miriam,

I told you I would keep writing until the day I died, but my hands are getting weak as I wait for Gavin to find his heart and come back to the house. It shouldn't be long now until I am beside you under your favorite trees. It's hard to believe we planted these trees together over 60 years ago. One for each child we lost. It's also hard to believe that I've spent 54 years without you. Sometimes I wake up and look over. I start talking to you like we always did. 6am conversations about nothing. I miss you and I can't wait to be beside you again. This life hasn't been an easy one without you.

As I come close to my own death I realize there are many good memories we shared. Too many. I can't seem to focus on those right now. What I really want to tell you in this last letter is that I'm sorry.

I'm sorry I stopped writing you these letters after Harold was born. You became so attached to him and I felt shoved aside. I should've kept writing. I hope I've made it up to you in the 2,592 letters I've written since you died.

I'm sorry for not being a good father. I didn't give him the attention he needed and I failed you too. I know I did. I'm sorry, Miriam. I took Gavin under my wing and treated him as though he were my own son. Really felt like he was too. Great kid. You'd be proud of him.

I'm sorry for realizing too late that life is too short to be stupid and selfish. I wasted too many minutes of our life together thinking about what I wanted to eat, or what I wanted to do. I should've asked you more. I should've loved you so much that I wanted only what you wanted.

I was young and stupid. You died before I got the chance to love you right. You always likened our romance to the garden. You said it needed lots of care every day. Water, but not too much water. Sun, but not too much sun. You said if we took care of it long enough the roots would strengthen and we would naturally thrive without so much attention to details. I'm afraid we never got to that point and it's my fault.

I love you, my Miriam. Always have, always will. My roots are strong now, but you've been ripped out of my garden. So I'm ready now, if you'll still have me, to be buried beside you.

And if anyone ever reads this letter (hello Gavin), do me a favor. Plant a garden over top of our graves. And anytime your own marriage faces trials, especially early on, come back to the garden and remember that the hard work is worth it.

Every love story has obstacles that make both people realize whether what they have is worth fighting for. So realize it now and always say I'm sorry, even when you didn't do anything wrong, just take the blame anyway. Remember, life is too short to be stupid. So spend your life loving.

Back to you, my Miriam, I'm coming now. It won't be long. I miss you so much.

I hereby proclaim the last love letter of thousands.

Most affectionately yours,
Edward Kessler

Snowflakes clung to Ella's scarf and our faces as I folded up the letter and set it back on the grave. Death has a funny way of making you realize how fragile your own life is. I turned to Ella and kissed her in the frosty November night. We created so much warmth that the snowflakes melted on our faces.

I picked her up and carried her up the snow-dusted hill to the house, our house. When I reached the top I slipped and fell on top of her. We laughed and laughed until we lost a few pounds. I hate the cold, absolutely loathe it, but with her by my side, I could've fallen asleep on those white hills without realizing I was freezing death. There was something beautiful, deeper. Something amazing about being able to call her my wife. It filled me in ways I never knew I needed to be filled.

"My dear wife," I said, then picked her up again. "You have bewitched me, body and soul, and I love, I love, I love you. I never wish to be parted from you from this day on."

She smiled. "You've been memorizing Jane Austen movies, huh?"

"I prefer Shakespeare though," I said, out of breath, as we reached the porch.

"Do you have Shakespeare memorized too?"

I kicked the door open and carried her up the stairs. "Love is not love which alters it when alteration finds, or bends with the remover to remove: O no! It is an ever fixed mark that looks on tempests and is never shaken; it is the star to every wandering bark whose worth's unknown, although his height be taken. Love's not Time's fool, though rosy lips and cheeks within his bending sickle's compass come: Love alters not with his brief hours and weeks, but bears it out, even to the edge of doom."

"Wow," she said, as I laid her on our bed. "You memorized all that?"

"I spent most of my life reading. Most guys quote Anchorman, I quote Shakespeare and Dickens."

"I prefer Shakespeare to Will Ferrell any day."

"And I prefer you over all the other flowers in the garden." I kissed her neck as she smiled.

"Even the roses?"

"Even the roses." I kept kissing.

"What kind of flower am I?"

"Easy," I said. "Middlemist red."

"What's that?"

"Look it up later." I kissed her lips. "For now, just kiss me."

I pulled the covers over our heads. We kissed until we could no longer breath. The sticky air between us cooled as I pulled the covers back. We embraced and kissed again, her hair climbing all over the milky-white pillows, for what felt like hours before we allowed our bodies to become one again.

The moonlight reflected from the carpet of snow outside, lighting up our room and projecting shadows of our bodies on the wall. And it was there, in that moment, that I realized I could get through any winter, any season of life, if I had this woman by my side. Not a woman in the world could compare to my wife. My one of a kind.

My middlemist red.

Continue to follow the stories of your favorite characters
from *The Unspoken Series* in Book 3,
written from the perspective's of Heidi and Patrick.

The Life I Now Live
November 19, 2013

Visit Marilyn-Grey.com *to vote on
the characters you'd like to read more
about in the next books.*

Your Questions Answered

Q. I love Gavin and Ella. Where did you come up with their characters? Are they based off of real people?

A. Yes, they are. I know a couple who lives and breathes romance. They truly are a beautiful couple inside and out. They love each other deeply, stick by each other through everything, and help each other grow. Gavin and Ella are a little different with their past and little nuances, but the overall tone and romance they share was based off of a real couple I am grateful to know.

Q. Do you plot out your stories before writing or figure it out as you go?

A. A little of both. I have a general idea for the beginning and ending of every story, then let it flow from there. My characters become so real to me. They become my friends. People I know and love. As I wrote from Ella and Matthew's perspectives in the first book I really tried to become them. Almost like acting, which I love. Same with Gavin for the second book. I stepped into his life and walked in his shoes. I let him show me how he felt, what he wanted to do, how he wanted to react. Sometimes he says and does things I don't agree with, but I have to let him do it anyway. I'm not him. I have to let him live on the page and become real. And because of that I definitely am surprised by a lot of the things that happen in the story. This ending wasn't what I expected. I thought they would get married in the hospital when Sarah was ready to be moved to the chapel there, but they surprised me and did it sooner.

Q. **Since you now live in Chicago, do you think you'll ever write about a character from there?**

A. Well, I grew up in Philadelphia and I love it there. Philly is home to me. I love Pennsylvania so much. I'll probably keep most of the series in Philly, but honestly, who knows! I'm willing to see where the next books take me and maybe I'll end up taking readers on a stroll through Paris! It's all a mystery to me too!

Q. **Which books have you completed so far?**

A. Only books 1 through 3. My publisher and I haven't decided yet which characters we'd like to focus on for books 4 through 6. I'm eager to pen Mwenye and Tylissa's story. Also Sarah and James. But Miranda has a great personality too. She will be a lot of fun. It's hard to choose! We have a voting poll set up on my website so that readers can decide which books they'd like to see first.

Q. **How many books in total will be in The Unspoken Series?**

A. I think we decided on 10 max, but we'll see how it goes. Everyone adores Gavin and Ella so I am hoping to end the series with them again. I love them so much too!

Q. **Writing any other series? Have any ideas?**

A. Yes, we have a few ideas brewing for another series. Considering a young adult series with high schoolers, but it hasn't been fleshed out enough yet.

Q. **Do you consider your books to be romance novels?**

A. I don't actually. They aren't heated or erotic. People who tend to look for high tension romance novels with shirts flying off every three seconds or villains that make you cringe probably won't like The Unspoken Series.

My writing is more character-driven. It's more internal. The characters struggle with life and learn to love in the process. It's not quite as angsty as some other romance novels out there. But I am who I am and my writing reflects that. I know it's not everyone's cup of tea and that's fine. As long as one person is touched by the story, that's worth it for me.

Q. How often do you write?

A. Every day. At least 2000 words. Most of the time more. I write constantly. My iPhone is synced with my iPad and iMac. Gotta love all these gadgets. I can write anywhere, anytime, and it syncs with all devices. So it's great. Makes it easier and when I'm inspired, no matter where I am (in line at the grocery store), I can start writing. I love that … although like Ella, I'm a little old-fashioned myself. I'd absolutely love to relive the 1800s alongside Ella.

If you have any questions you'd like to see answered in the next book, please email them to Marilyn at **marilyn@marilyn-grey.com** *and we'll select some to answer. You will also receive an answer from her via email. She responds to every email from fans.*

www.ingramcontent.com/pod-product-compliance
Lightning Source LLC
Chambersburg PA
CBHW021057130626
46552CB00005B/2155